Warrior Woman

"I will have a band of the most beautiful fighters ever seen in the area," said Ifania. "If Gyre produced Zadieyek, I have no doubt there are other fighting women who could be induced to come and exhibit their skills!"

I stared at Ifania in astonishment and dismay. I wished to be free of the arena, not to seduce others into it. But Ifania's friends all joined in with excitement at the thought that women fighters might come to dominate the arena. I do not know why the thought pleases them so much. What, I wonder, in the name of any or all of the Gods, excites them in the idea of women fighting in the gladiatorial spectacle? Do they not know that I would change my life with any of them? Do they think I chose this life because I liked it?

D1425187

Also in Arrow by Marion Zimmer Bradley

THE DARKOVER NOVELS

Warrior Woman

Marion Zimmer Bradley

A Darkover novel

ARROW BOOKS

Arrow Books Limited
62–65 Chandos Place, London WC2N 4NW

An imprint of Century Hutchinson Limited

London Melbourne Sydney Auckland
Johannesburg and agencies throughout
the world

First published in Great Britain 1987

Printed and bound in Great Britain by
Anchor Brendon Limited, Tiptree, Essex

ISBN 0 09 949310 1

PROLOGUE

In the days before man traveled space, there were those who sat in elegant control rooms, guiding satellites into orbit or giant robots to construct buildings or master computers to affect decisions across a continent or a world. And also there were those who wandered the desert of the outback, barefoot and with no possessions except a waterskin and a throwing stick, hunting sipwells and gathering roots, and those who pushed wooden plows with their bare hands and prayed to strange gods for rain.

Beyond our world lie a million billion suns lighting a million billion other worlds, and uncountable men and women struggling to live and thrive. And on some of them men build cities, and dwell in them served by giant brains and robots, and on others men struggle to survive in desert or virgin forest, with sword and throwing-stick and whatever powers their un-known gods have given to their bodies and their minds.

So it is.

So will it be ever, worlds without end.

1

White fire explodes around me. A blow splits my head.

Heat. Pain. I gasp, suffocate for eternities, die.

Rough hands suddenly on me. I am not dead, dimly I know this; I struggle against the hands, not knowing if they are intending to help or hurt; I suffocate again, words meant to soothe have no meaning; time is gone; the hands tearing my skirt, parting my thighs, I am naked, an animal biting, sobbing, suffocating without breath to scream, fighting to run, claw, tear, bite, survive.

I am held, forced; I howl, suffocate, fighting for breath, a naked animal, fighting, fighting, if only for breath to scream again. A fierce face, ugly, ugly, bearded, tearing away the last rag of clothing. I am split, torn, bleeding; will this

*agony never be finished? pain and terror, I
fight, claw, bleed, suffocate.*

*A blow splits my head. White fire explodes
around me.*

And I wake screaming. Again.

"Jasric, God of warriors," someone groans in
the suffocating dark, "keep that damned girl
quiet for once. We've all got nightmares. Shut
up, you."

I shift my chains on rough stone, huddle my
chains around me, try to sleep.

White fire splits my head. . . .

My first real memory, pain, endless jolting. Even
now in nightmares I remember pain, jolting,
tied to the back of some animal, but concepts
like *pain, jolting, animal, tied,* these have no
meaning for me. I have no language to describe
them. I suffer endlessly, not knowing why or
how, a hurt animal. I do not know what has
happened to me; everything before this has been
burned clean in white fire. I do not know what
memory is or that I have lost it. That all comes
later. I sleep exhausted, wake, am allowed to
eat and drink (but never enough) and too often
when I wake, before food or drink, hands fumbling with me, the weight and demand of someone whose face I try never to see while I fight
and scream knowing that if I fight too hard
there will be no food and, worse, no water.
Afterward, always afterward, I am tied again,
struggling, to some animal. After a time I learn

the tying means me no harm and longer fight
against the tying, the animal; but even though I
know it may mean hunger and thirst, I can
never make myself stop fighting the men's hands
and bodies, striking out, clawing, cursing. I tell
myself that when it is over it will mean food
and water but I cannot force myself to bear *that*
with patience. Later, I am allowed to ride. I
learn simple words: saddle, ride, hurt, food,
thirsty, sleep. *Thirsty* is the commonest; I am
always thirsty.

Then, cleanly surfacing into my mind: I am
in a great stone-floored room, with a great stone
basin filled to the brim with water. I remember
trying to drink the water of the pool, and there
is kind laughter before a drinking vessel is held
to my lips and for the first time in memory I
am allowed to quench my thirst, though twice I
pause, cringing, waiting for a blow to stop the
drinking and the vessel to be wrenched away
from me. Some time later I am given a bath, the
water heavenly to my burnt and tormented skin.
Afterward there are skilled fingers kneading
my muscles, and ointments to soothe the hurts
of days in the saddle.

It seems to me that there are days and nights
in this place, the first peace I have ever known.
No longer, when it grows dark, am I taken from
the saddle and left where hands can fumble at
me in the dark and blows stifle my screams; I
have never learned not to scream or to fight.
Here there are women to guard us, and I can
sleep without that particular terror, but it is

here that I learn another word, *nightmare*, for the waking out of sleep to white fire splitting my head, suffocation, fighting, clawing, dying. I learn it is not happening again, that it is only a bad dream, but I am afraid to sleep, and learn another word. *Fear.*

One of the days there is a woman to bathe me again, combing and dressing my long hair; I cry as she jerks at the tangles and instead of quieting me with blows she cuts the knots in the long locks with a knife and soothes me with soft words I am beginning to know. I lean into her arms, sob against her breast and she holds me. I am happy. I want it to go on forever, but gently she prods me to sit upright so she can finish the combing and dress me in a brief gown, too short, I try to jerk it over my knees but it will not cover my long legs, while the other women laugh at me and tease me in words I do not know. I am dressed and scented, and given wine which burns my mouth; the other women laugh again when I splutter it out, but the kind one holds it again to my lips, gently insisting that I drink it all. To please her I swallow the hot fire in my mouth, cough and splutter down the front of my gown, but the kind woman stops the one who curses and tries to strike me, and brings a cloth to wipe away the stain. Then, as I fight and sob, chains are fastened again around my wrists and I am pushed out in a long line of other men and women, displayed on a high stage.

And then I know I am to be sold as a slave.

I think now that I must have understood more words than I realized, that I must know, a little, what is happening as I stand on the block, cries and calls too fast for me to hear. I shrink, trying to cover myself with the inadequate shift around my body. I hear laughter and do not know they are mocking me.

Sooner or later I am pushed toward a buyer. I have no idea of my price but I think it must have been high. With two other women and a couple of rough-looking men in chains, I am led to a litter and shoved inside. I wonder if the unaccustomed wine, which is still making my head wobble and my sight blear, will make me throw up all over the fine cushions of the litter. The litter sways under me, through the rough stone streets. The other women tell me that we have been sold as whores to the Master of Gladiators. I do not know what this means. But one of the men, a brute in a leather apron, comes to me and tries to pull aside my dress. I whimper, and a sharp word stops him.

"Get back to your place, man! There'll be time enough for that later, when you've earned it. Oh, they treat you fine in the Gladiator's School, food enough and wine, even women—didn't he buy these three? But it's for the Master to say when and where you get to use the women, so hands off for now, hear me? That's orders." And the brute lets me go.

And then the litter stops and all of us, the other women, the brute in the leather apron, a tall frightened-looking boy not more than sev-

enteen, are pushed out into a vast indoor courtyard. Weapons are piled up in heaps and hung
on the walls of the buildings that surround us.
At one end there is a bathing pool, and a building I later learn to be a fine bath house. At the
other end was what (I later learned) we call the
Doorway to Fate, for it leads into the Arena
from which so many of us never return. At the
other sides are living quarters and a forge where
weapons are made.

In the courtyard half a dozen men are working out with swords and spears; others are in
the middle of a slow dancelike exercise. All
activity stops as the litter comes to a halt, and
they crowd around to look at us. But the memory of the sound of clashing metal is in my
ears, and I stare at the swords on the walls. I
feel my fingers curving and clenching, aching
for the feel of one of them in my palm, my
hand is actually poised for the grip of the hilts.

The men crowd around the litter with a cry
of "Women!" As we descend, they make good-
natured cat-calls of welcome at the brute with
the muscles, at the terrified adolescent. "Hey,
what's that, gladiator or a bedbug for those as
can't manage with the women?" He shrinks
and I am sorry for him, but then he grabs up
one of the swords from the wall and gestures
with it and there is a good-natured cheer of
welcome.

But there are other sounds, words I hardly
understand, for the other women, and for me,
when we descend. I know we have been bought

for the use of these most brutish of men, and between the unused wine in my belly and my fear, I think I will be sick again.

One of the men, still holding a sword casually on one arm, comes to the smallest and prettiest of the women, who reaches up to pat his ugly cheek and smile engagingly at him. He pulls her toward the door of what I later know are the sleeping quarters. A man I will soon know as the Master of Gladiators nods permission and jerks his head at one of the favored men. He comes to me, takes a crude hold of my breasts, and as I flinch backward, says something too gross for my limited language. There is rough laughter, jeers as he pulls away the skirt that does not properly cover me.

And I know that this is the moment of choice. If I back down now, if I let him take me toward that room, I will spend what remains of my life spreading my legs for these brutes. . . .

White fire splitting my head, a blow, scream, suffocate, die, a naked animal fighting hands that part my thighs—

Better to die quickly. With one leap the sword is in my hand, my palm curves around it like an old friend. Sick, drunk, my body remembering what I do not, I fall into what I later know to be the classic pattern of defense. I use both hands on the sword; they are still manacled together and I have no choice.

With a howl of rage he raises his own sword, and I—sick, drunk, manacled—I split his skull.

"Jasric guard us! The wench is a warrior!" It is

the voice of the Master of Gladiators. He strides to me through the silence around us. The last woman has been tittering nervously, falls silent as he glares at her.

He jerks his head. "Get her the key."

Someone tosses me a key. Without letting go of the sword. I bend my head and wrench the key in my teeth toward the manacles. At a signal from the Master of Gladiators, someone—I do not look at his face—comes to twist the key and set me free.

The Master Gladiators says, "I don't usually bother with woman gladiators. They're more trouble than they're worth. But you've earned the right to a trial. Want it? Believe me, girl, whoring's an easier life." And he waits for my answer. There is no sound at all except water splashing in the fountain at the far end of the courtyard. Even the other harlot has stopped her giggling.

My voice is thick, rusty with disuse, and I have little of the language, but I struggle for the words.

"I am no harlot. If I must be one or the other, I a fighter will be."

"Your right, then, to choose," he says, and gestures; two of the men drag away the body of the man I have killed. I never find out who he was, not even his name. The Master looks at the remaining girl and stands, belligerently, arms akimbo.

"You going to fight for a chance at the sword?"

She shakes her head, backs away, glaring at me with real hate. I don't know why.

"So. Two whores are enough for the rest of you loafing cowards. Enough time wasted." He nods at one of the men, who takes away the last of the women, and glares at me.

"You, girl. Pick yourself a sword over there . . . or do you like that one? I'd say it's heavy for you, but work with it and see how it goes. I'll find someone to work out with you." His eyes sweep quickly around the ring of men. He says with quiet menace, "Remember; she's a fighter, not one of your whores. Hands off. Girl, I give you leave to protect yourself, but no killing, remember."

So I become a gladiator.

2 | Cold water splashes my face; my hands, callused now, scrape runnels of sweat and grime from my body.

"Splash a little my way, Zad'yek," Hassim grunts, and I raise a bucket, sending it washing over his moonface, the broad shoulders bearing the scars of a lifetime spent in heavy armor: the brown stains of leather harness on front and back and round his waist. Intermingled with the patterns made on his body by armor are healed white slashes from half a hundred cuts. I do not know whether they are the scars of battle or of the arena. I do not care. They are the scars of a survivor. He can help me.

"Whoosh! Good, Zad'yek." He signals for another bucket. This is the work of the trainer, but I oblige him, cascading another pail of water over his sweating carcass.

Zad'yek; it is what they call me now. It is not a name, but I have no other. Zad'yek. A slurred form of Zadieyek which means, in their language, something like *dreaded woman*.

Hassim blinks comically as he fingers water from his face, groaning with pleasure at the coolness. Then he picks up the drinking bucket, and takes a sparing, almost a dainty drink. Already he has taught me this, by wrenching the bucket from me when I would have drunk deep. (Still the memory of the desert thirst torments me. Once he let me drink my fill, then grunted in sympathy and patted my back through the agonizing cramps that followed.

He settles on the floor as I take careful sips from the drinking bucket, then pulls me down beside him.

"You're not a gladiator yet, girl. Long work ahead, much to learn. Rest the muscles. Overtrain, you get sick, get killed first time out past Doorway of Doom." They call it this too, as well as Doorway of Fate.

Hassim speaks in short grunting phrases, this language not native to him either. I ponder this, trying to take my memory back as far as it will go (*Jolting. White fire in my brain . . .*) and give it up.

I have learned enough to know how little I know. A woman my age would never have mother or father, sisters, brothers, friends, kinfolk. Husband or lover. Even if born a slave, some master would have claimed me before I came into the slave market of this city, which I now know is called Jemmok. I know I was brought a long way across the desert, bound and captive and chained on the back of some animal; but I do not even know the direction from which I was brought, nor do I bear marks of previous chaining.

Hassim never asks. Does not care. The first time they send him to work out with me he scowls, bearlike, hearing the jeers of the men. The leather-aproned brute has been sent to work the bellows of the forge where weapons are made or mended; the long-legged boy is being instructed by the Master of Gladiators himself. But I know enough, not knowing how I know, to feel gratitude for the luck of the draw which puts me in Hassim's hands. He has a real passion for weapons and never tires of talking about them, even when we fling ourselves down for the permitted half-timestick of rest mid-afternoon and midmorning.

The other men talk of wine, women, old friends dead beyond the Doorway of Fate, the gold sometimes lavished on a successful gladiator by a rich person.

Hassim speaks only of fighting, of weapons.

"Keep that shield-arm up, girl, I could have got in past you this morning. Strengthen it. We get you a shield pointed—" he gestures, "like weapon on bottom, good weapon, slam it down, better as spear. Better as sword, you see, but shield-arm not strong like sword-arm yet. We build arm like rock. Look." He puts his massive left arm, tightening his fist, into my hand.

"Strong like bull. Cow be strong too, hah!" But his hands on my arm do not offend me. He touches me as he touches a weapon, but with less tenderness.

"I'll practice," I promise, and haul my weary body upright. The trainer comes to inspect the shield as Hassim pulls it down for me.

"Too heavy for you, isn't it, girl?"

I shake my head, knowing somewhere inside myself that a lighter shield will not balance when I throw my weight forward, committing my body to the powerful impulse of the joined strike of shield and sword. I take it by the point, throw it up so that it tumbles end over end in the air, and catch it by the handle. My body remembers doing this; I do not. I say clumsily, stumbling for words, "Way to choose shield, in my country. This one good, balance right."

"Oh?" His eyes linger on me, curious. "Where's your country?"

Blankness overcomes me again and I clench my jaw against frightened tears.

"I—I can't remember."

He shrugs. I don't know whether he believes me or whether he doesn't really care.

"Hassim. Teach her to use the shield."

Ten days. Ten days, then either I die beyond the Doorway of Fate, or I am a true gladiator, under protection of the Akharet—the ruler of the City, the Great All-Powerful—while I live. A slave, but a very special slave. Most buy their freedom within three years, if they live. Many retire rich. Many remain. Like Hassim, it has become a passion with them. I work till I tremble, but always, when I fall exhausted into sleep. . . .

White fire splits my brain, I suffocate, scream, fight for breath to scream again, feel my body split asunder by what I now have knowledge enough to call rape, wake screaming. . . .

Hassim is kneeling beside me, his heavy familiar presence under my blankets. I tense to push him away; he gentles me with impersonal hands as with an animal.

"No? I think, make pleasure, drive away . . ." he too fumbles, not knowing the word, "drive out nightmare." But he feels my tense held-breath terror. This is my friend, surely he should have from me what I could not keep others from taking. But that was in the darkness of nightmare, pre-memory. He feels me shaking. "No? Sure not? Here, then, put your head on my shoulder. Sleep, girl, sleep quiet or they beat us for making noise, now."

He holds me. As a father. Had I ever a father? What do I know of that? No. As a child his favorite toy, as Hassim holds his best sword: Tenderly, possessive, careful to avoid damage.

I sleep and for once do not wake.

Little by little, in the days before the Games, I learn.

The city is Jemmok, ruled by the Akharet, the All-Powerful, and his consort. I am not sure whether she is his sister or his wife or perhaps both, the subtleties of this language still defeat me at times. The Akharet and his consort each own a *tammarim*, a fourteen, of gladiators; mimicking them, each noble in Jemmok, both men and women, bid on such warriors as the Akharet or his consort do not choose. It is best to be owned by the Akharet. After my trial in the Arena, I will be put up for lot, if either the Akharet or his consort seek me; if not, the nobles may bid for me.

With status as a gladiator, there are laws to protect me. I may not be used as a harlot nor sold as one. I may be killed only in the Arena; there are dreadful penalties for killing a gladiator except in the arena with the permitted weapons. If I had not been ready to die, I would never have dared to fight that man who touched me on that first day; only luck prompted me to snatch the sword and split his skull. Because I took, by instinct, the sword, I won a chance to a trial in the arena. If I had, for instance, split his skull with my manacles, I would have been tortured, or burnt, or turned over to the men until I was dead, then my body flung on the swill-pile for the pigs to devour.

Four days before the contests which open the new Games, which have a name and a purpose I never learn, I am told that I am to be paired for my first fight with a newcomer, a tall whippy man, with hanks of red hair and a long scar distorting his mouth, who fights with net

and trident. I fear no man at swordplay, but at
night I wake in terror, not, this time, of white
fire and suffocation and rape, but of the terrible
barbed bite of the trident into my flesh.

And the day comes, with braying of trumpets
so loud that the City must be full of it. The
gladiators are given a bath, and roast fowl, and
plenty of wine, which I do not touch because it
burns my mouth and I know I will only throw
it up again. The fighters of the Akharet are
dressed in new tunics of crimson with gold
trim, and those belonging to the consort in
lavish purple. Each noble sends fourteen new
tunics for his tammarin of fighters. Those of us
virgin to the arena and not as yet belonging to
anyone are clothed in stiff new white linen and
paraded behind the other, owned gladiators
through the Doorway of Fate. I look at Hassim
in his purple tunic and fail to recognize the
familiar face. It is all unreal, everything is unreal, as I am unreal.

Beyond the Doorway of Fate great lights burst
in my eyes and I hear a great sound like a
distant ocean, or like the roar of . . . the roar of
. . . almost I know what that sound is, before I
know it is the noise of the crowd, battering at
our ears, screaming out at us in greeting. Hate,
love, lust for blood, or a little of all of these?
Hassim warned me the night before:

*"Never look at the crowd. Nothing for you,
nothing exists but you and your opponent in
the arena. Never look up even at your patron,*

not even if your patron is your lover. Especially not if your patron is your lover."

Paraded once round the Arena so that everyone can see us, then we are drawn up according to our specialties. I glance at Hassim, suddenly terrified, but he does not glance my way. I am on my own, wholly on my own, he has his own life-or-death battle to fight and he cannot think of me, as I must not let my mind dwell on him. I still feel unreal, that I will have to fight, yet my body remembers what my mind does not and I brace myself, the cold taste of metal in my mouth, and I suddenly feel as if I must run to empty my bladder, or I will wet my clothes like a little girl, or that I must run off the field in panic. Yet through and over all these things, I know I will not do any of them; I curve my palm around the hilt of my sword and know that my wrists are hardened steel, that I am ready to raise the sword.

But they are not yet ready for me. First there is a combat between the tall adolescent who had been trained by the Master of Gladiators himself and a small yellow-skinned fellow I have not often seen in the training room, armed with a sling and a short knife. It looks like murder, pitting this little man against the tall heavy-muscled lad with his long sword and pointed shield like mine. The little sling-fighter is naked except for a loincloth and a small metal helmet, while the swordsman bears leather armor like mine.

The sling-fighter circles, like a scuttling crab.

I see that he does not wear a white linen tunic as do the other fighters virgin to the Arena, and wonder, for the loincloth is colorless, whether he is an amateur, or an owned gladiator of some nobleman's *tammarin*.

I hear the crowd-roar swell to a scream. The sling-fighter, then, is the favorite. I watch the white-clad novice, my brother-in-arms, whose name I don't know, as he keeps turning to face the sling-fighter's scuttling rushes. So swiftly that I cannot see his arm move, the sling-fighter whirls his small weapon and I hear something go *Thwack!* on the swordsman-novice's shield. A second follows it, and this one I do not hear, but the white-clad youth, with am almost inaudible groan of pain, drops the shield. As he fumbles for it the sling-fighter makes another quick rush, and as the swordsman straightens his eye explodes into a crimson shower, and he goes down with a scream of anguish. Before he can recover himself or straighten, the sling-fighter sends another whirling stone and a black hole appears in the forehead above the ruined eye. The young swordsman, blood pouring over his virgin tunic, goes down and does not rise. The sling-fighter flings up his arms with a raucous cheer and the crowds go mad.

Murder, then, but not as I thought. It was the long-muscled novice with shield and sword who was helpless as a child before the sling-fighter. Later I learn that the sling-fighter is allowed only a *tammarin*, fourteen, of his smooth deadly stones; once they are exhausted, he can be hunted down and butchered, having no defense, except for the finger-long knife, hardly long enough for cutting meat at table. But let his opponent's shield slip for an instant, or expose head or vitals for a moment, and death is swift. The white-clad boy will never have a chance to learn this. I watch, beyond horror, beyond caring.

Now it is my name they are calling, Zadieyek, *Dreaded woman*. My hands are like lead and it is hard to pick up my feet. I remind myself: the worst my net-fighter opponent can do is to kill me; cowardice in the arena is rewarded with torture. Yet there is such a sour taste in my mouth, such a quaking in my bladder, that for a moment I am afraid I will vomit or soil myself there before the entire crowd.

A merciful moment of respite is given to me by the crowd's applause. I know I am beautiful, I know the men there would like to tumble me and because they cannot, they will settle for seeing blood drawn from the pale skin, red streaks staining white loin-cloth, the breasts that they might not touch battered and bleeding. I know the women will scream for blood drawn from legs longer and shapelier than their own, wounds to the waist smaller than theirs.

I don't grudge them the cruelty of that need for blood, it gives me a moment of needed respite, so I can strengthen my calm against that sea of mindless faces who have come to see me mangled and murdered.

Then I forget them again. I hear only a distant roar like the beating of surf on a faraway beach (*what is surf? What is a beach?*) while I am again aware of the white sand scattered to drink up my blood, this place which is the only place I have really known, and which now may be the place of my death.

Coldly I size up the red-haired man who stands leering at the crowd, net gathered into one hand with careless ease. His lips move. Is he praying?

No. Muttering words; words directed at me, words which bring me all the way back to the realities of this place.

"Stand still, girl, and I'll finish you off quick, no grudge, neck instead of guts; you don't want to be a long time dying on a day like this. I have enough prestige I can get away with it."

I say between my teeth "You'd like that? Go to hell. Fight, man."

"So be it." His accent, barbarous as mine, spits between clenched teeth, from the faraway North or so they say. "Your choice, if I have to do a crowd-pleaser, spin it out a long time, hurt you. They like that. Just don't beg me *then* to make it quick, bitch."

"No fear," I say, and curl my lip in contempt. He is trying to get the upper hand of me, no more, I know it in my heart as we break and square off at opposite ends of that imaginary circle drawn in the white glare of the sand. I watch his hands tighten on the net and it comes loose and flies at me, a pale immense cloud, and I break and run, watchful as it settles down, a great spider's web hovering. If I have miscalculated it will drop over me. . . .

No. I am safely beyond its perimeter, it lies billowing on the sand for a moment before it collapses and falls inert; he breaks and runs for it as I hear a great surge of sound go up from the faraway surf. Disappointment? Pleasure that the newcomer has escaped, that the fight will be longer, not a swift perfunctory butchery like the last? He is lightning fast, he will gather it up and cast again, but this is my moment, my free cast to prevent him. I run, circling the net's edge, and for the moment when he stoops to gather it in, one hand wary on the great trident, I make one sweep down with my sword, hacking at the arm bearing the net.

He howls, pain or rage I am not sure, and the trident hurtles, but my second blow has spoiled his arm and the trident falls short. I back off and watch it drop; for an instant I want to rush in and finish him off with the sword, but I have been cautioned about this, at close range I would have no chance against the net.

Even before the trident hits dirt he has gathered up the net in both hands, this time, and scuttles away, a long-legged spider with one arm pouring blood. The net is a whirling cloud high over his head; it comes flying. I dance away, but one weighted edge strikes my shoulder—I had no idea how heavy it was—and cuts like a knife. For a moment, dizzied, I fumble my sword, knowing my other arm is caught in the net. He is on me, in a great whirling rush.

The barbed trident seems to blot out the sky above, to come at me slowly, so slowly, as the noise of the surf batters at my ears.

Then the sword is part of my hand again, and I stab upward, awkward, awkward, the net still tangling my other arm. The trident stabs home in my thigh. Strangely it does not hurt, I see it go in and hear the crowd screaming, but I hack upward again at that arm holding the trident, clumsy butchery across the great muscle of the arm. The arm clutching the trident flies upward, muscles in spasm, the barb jerks free, ripping my thigh in a broad gash, still painless, and he howls, clawing at the net. I lop at the net-arm, forcing myself forward, feel my sword go through the arm, follow through into his chest, where it skids on bone and turns. It is so heavy now, I feel so heavy, but I haul the sword upward and deliver one more clumsy chop to his thick neck. He sinks down, his mouth rounded in the terrible O of a scream I cannot hear through the pounding surf. I must manage one more blow, this the death-blow, as he thrashes and lies still, a last gush of blood coming and stopping. Dizzied, I stand beside him, not yet aware that I have survived my first fight, that it is over and I am not to die today.

As I have seen the others do, I fling my arm up to the sea-surging crowds, saluting them with a dizzied exaltation. Suddenly I am very hungry and I can think only of the roasting meat and honey-cakes awaiting the survivors beyond the gates. I feel a terrible burning in my thigh and become aware that it is still oozing blood. It hurts so fiercely that I want to cry like a little girl who has skinned her knee. But, blinking fiercely, I keep back the tears.

Zad'yek, *dreaded woman*, that is now who I am, can a dreaded woman cry like a little girl who has fallen and skinned her knee?

3 That night as I sit among them, gnawing at a last bone, a stray cake sticky with nuts and honey, a messenger comes seeking me, calling out my name. This has happened before but only for two or three of the men who are great public favorites. The messenger stands gawking at us where we sit on our cushions, bathed and combed and dressed and curled and a million light-years from the death-stink and blood on the other side of the Doorway of Doom.

"For Zadieyek, the warrior woman," he says, and gabbles the name of some noble. "She begs you to dine at her house and accept these worthless trifles to adorn yourself should you choose to celebrate your victory at her table."

I want to fling the worthless trifles at his feet but I remember I have need of clothing other than the city-given fighting tunic; of sandals, of creams for my skin, callused by armor. I bow and say "Tell your mistress that I am grateful and I shall remember her name, but tell her I have dined already."

From the messenger's face I know he has heard this excuse many times already; nevertheless he insists on leaving the "worthless trifles" for my acceptance.

"So, you have found a patron," Hassim says, and informs me that my new patron is a wealthy lady who desires to establish her own *tammarim*. She will probably, Hassim suggests, offer to buy my contract; while this is pending, it is etiquette for me to accept gifts of clothing, money, and delicacies and the acceptance commits me to nothing, although if I join another's *tammarim* it is customary to return expensive jewelry. "Now let us see how she values you, Zad'yek," Hassim suggests, and we open the bundle, discoving that the "worthless trifles" are a bundle of beautifully dyed silk lengths for tunics, each with its own silken cord, woven or braided; an enamelled box containing sticks and tiny pots—cosmetics, all suited to my coloring, many of which I do not know how to apply; and two small pairs of dyed leather sandals. I feel like a child at a birthday party *(what is a birthday?)* I wonder, with a picture somewhere in my mind of children wearing silly hats and watching fireworks and opening packages like these, a picture from somewhere *behind* the white fire and the desert and the thirst.

Twice more this evening my name is called and some messenger delivers me gifts, once a great basket of fruits and once a casket of jewels. Now I have sandals and clothing and cosmetics and gilt nets for my hair and smoothing oils and perfumes to keep the stench of death from my nostrils.

Hassim, the next day, counsels me how to care for my new wealth, a trusty agent in the city. "Pay him a good commission. Make him rich if you live, make sure he gets nothing if you die, else he can have you drugged or poisoned.

Hassim bears a wound from the day's fighting. He makes light of it, insisting he has had worse from practice, and examines my gifts one by one.

"This," he says, taking up a glittering crescent with pretty stones, "you wear; small enough not to hinder you, flash enough to make good impression in arena—good that you be known to have admirers, be popular; some day you need crowd goodwill, discourage the one you fight. This—" a box of elaborate cakes and sweetmeats— "you share with all gladiators; do you no harm to be known as popular, generous. These—" he examines a packet of expensive sticky sweetmeats— "give to slaves. You eat, belly clogged, skin break out; but give to slaves and harlots, make them happy, good to be popular with them. These—" he opened the jeweled box, revealing a string of pearls fit for the throat of the Akharet's consort— "these you sell."

To wear them, he counsels, would be to make a commitment to the noble who sent them. But to sell them, even though I keep the sale price, curiously commits me to nothing.

I do not understand these people.

His own patron has sent Hassim a jug of good wine which we drink as he counsels me; I still do not like it, and prefer to eat the fruits in my gift basket. Hassim reaches over and helps himself to a handful of grapes, ripe and green and juicy. For a time I watch sweat beads collect on his broad brown forehead and the bands of muscles across his cheek which I admire as a fighter, not as a woman. I wish I could accept him, give him the pleasure his kindness deserves. He does not, I suppose, want me that way, with the gritted teeth of endurance.

I decide to bestow the sweets on the woman who crossed the desert with me and chose harlotry over the fight for the arena. I have to wait to see her; she is with someone. When he comes out strutting and goes away she greets me with surprise and, I think, she is not displeased to see me.

"I heard that a woman gladiator had triumphed in the arena. Was it you, then? And you look well and fit." She accepts the delicacies with gratitude. "So kind of you to think of me. But how can you fight as you do? I would die of terror—surely you are beautiful enough that you could find a rich patron to care for you, you need not risk your life that way—"

"Then I would be no better than you," I blurt

out. "I could not give myself to all comers that way!"

Now she looks angry, challenged.

"At least it is a woman's way; I have not left off being a woman, I do not show my legs in the arena and let all men use me with their eyes in the arena without pay!"

There is justice, I know, in what she says, yet I know I would rather risk death in the arena than live as she does, enduring men's hands and their bodies. I am sorry she is angry with me, I would like to know what it is in her that will let her accept that touch, that brutality, without fighting to the death. Her next customer is waiting and as I leave he eyes me with that swagger and says, "I would rather have you, beautiful. I have an opal the size of a bird's egg; it is yours for an hour in my bed."

"I thank you for the offer" I say, knowing that what I really desire is to kill him for looking at me or thinking of me that way. How is it that he cannot see it as insult? "But I have no desire for jewels," I say, and he comes and pleads with me, raising the offer to a point where I can only laugh helplessly.

"You would give such a price for my body, even unwillingly given?"

"Willing or unwilling makes no difference to a man, beautiful one," he says, and I find it impossible to believe, remembering Hassim, saying that what is no pleasure to me is none to him. Yet he adds "I am gambling that with me you would find more pleasure than you have ever known," and I want to laugh, knowing I would not. Now the look of pleading changes to hostility, and I know that if he cannot have me he would like to see me killed in the arena or tortured.

I am bidden to dine with my new patron, and I am eager to go outside the training house where I have been since I came to this city. With a few coins from my new wealth I bribe the woman who waits on the harlots to wash and curl my hair, and set forth with two guards from the House of Fate to escort me through the city of which I have seen nothing; ostensibly so that no harm will come to me, but, I know, truly so that I will not escape. Pampered entertainers of the city that we may be, we are as truly slaves as the hobbled men who sweep filth from the city's gutters. Yet as I travel through the streets I see the city poorly organized for defense, I see gates which could be stormed by a few poorly armed men. I check off routes of escape, note a caravan leaving with guards—when I am ready to escape this city, as I know I am not yet ready, that would be the best way to go, hire out to guard a caravan ready to cross the desert that I remember only for the torture of thirst. Why does my brain keep clicking off these details compulsively? I am a gladiator, I have no wish or need to escape.

My patron, a soft-bodied lady who nevertheless looks as if once she had been herself a fighter, greets me and makes a fuss over me, seating me next to her at table, and feeding me choice bits from her plate, filled with a thousand questions about the world of the gladiators which I do not know how to answer.

"And have you a lover there, my dear? Once I heard of a woman who sold herself to the arena to pay her lover's debts," she says, and her eyes are moist with curiosity, her hands brush my body with a little more than just kind attention. After what I have endured in the desert the sight of desire in a woman's eyes does not frighten me, I do not push away her hands, which rove more freely as they are not rebuffed; the touches I find neither unpleasant nor threatening, and I feel a kind of power swell within me, the awareness of her desire, but what is it that she wishes from me? I am not repelled; I simply do not understand, though I reassure her that I have no lover in the House of Fate. Hassim is kindly and strong—as is the bond growing between us—but a lover he is not.

The days pass quietly with nothing to mark them; no one counts, but by the pace of training I know they are moving to another of the great festivals. One morning as I am caring for the new leather armor I have been given by my patron's generosity, I hear an outraged roar and go to see the commotion.

"Hands off, swine of Jemmok! Are there no harlots in this city, that you lay hands on an honest working woman?"

She is tall and strongly built with red hair in

two braids each as thick as my wrists, great
bands of muscle across the pectorals, breasts
that could never have been large and now were
all but buried in the bands of muscle. Waist
surprisingly small for her sturdy height and
broad shoulders. She moves on long muscular
legs, as smoothly as a jungle cat. The sturdy
man we all call "the Bull" emerges spluttering
like a fish from the water trough where she has
thrown him.

Her eyes rest on me. "I know not there was
another woman warrior here," she says. "Sister, are you of Gyre?"

"They tell me so; I know not. My memory is
gone."

"It must be so; only in Gyre do women take
the field as warriors," the red-haired woman
says. I wonder, longing for this faraway land of
Gyre where none will stare or wonder to see a
woman under arms.

The Master of Gladiators calls to me. "Zadieyek, take her in hand, show her around. Be
complimented, girl, it was you showed me a
woman can be more of a draw than the men, if
handled right."

I come forward, admiring her leather armor
studded with copper rivets, the vambraces that
rise to her elbows, the metal-banded greaves on
her sturdy legs, which look more adept at danc-
ing than fighting. A yellow silk chemise which
had once been fine guards her body from the
armor. There are scars on her body from years
of rubbing by armor, patches discolored by the

leather; rubbed and healed, rubbed and healed again.

"Zadieyek," she says, "but that is not a name. What was your name in Gyre, girl?"

"I remember no other name," I say to her meekly, and she laughs. "You have the hair and eyes of a woman of Satyang on the border, but there was a war there with many women as booty, and if you are Satyang, how would it be that you remember nothing but the sword? I heard never that any Satyang woman was warrior-trained." She laughed her great laughter. "Will you fight me for the right to the name Zadieyek, since I have as good a right to it as you?"

I do not want to fight her; I would rather be her friend, but dare I risk friendship here in the House of Doom? "Aye, I will fight you," I said. "You have another name to which you have a right; I have nothing that is mine save the name Zadieyek, which I won fairly in combat and will defend if I must."

She clasps me close in a great hug. "Keep the name, girl, your valor deserves it. I am Beizun. Where can I throw my gear, and where can a girl take a piss without all these whore's delights hanging around gawking?"

Such language from a woman I have never heard; next to her our harlots are fair-spoken and ladylike. Yet it seems to suit her flamboyant personality.

"Come along," I offer, "and I'll show you

where your weapons will be safe if you want to store them in safety."

So my friend Beizun comes to the House of Fate.

A rich woman, her eyes traced with kohl, comes to watch us in the training room and her eyes follow Hassim. I listen to the cooing voice, and a sick jealousy sends acid spurting into my throat. But this is madness; I do not want his muscular body, and she all too obviously wants nothing else. He comes, when we break for coarse roast meat and coarser boiled vegetables, to shave himself carefully, and the men, observing that he does not touch the bread and beer, shout taunts and cat-calls: "Too good for our vittles, Hassim, when you'll get roast fowl and sweetmeats with lady Silken-arse?"

He comes back late at night, stomping proudly across the floor, and in the light of the torch held high by the guard I see that he glitters with gold, a torque and bracelets wider than my new golden ornaments. When he lies down in his accustomed place beside me, I smell the rich scent of perfumed fards and through the rich attars I breathe in the heavy odor of wine, oozing from his very pores. When light comes he does not waken and at last I pour a bucket of water over him; he comes up choking and gasping like a great fish. I laugh callously at the groans as he moves about with his head carefully balanced on his shoulders as if it would fall off.

"Take care, Hassim" —one of the trainers

makes a crude joke— "Pour out all your strength through the Pillar of Fire, and you'll have none left and Old Bloody (death, I remember, the crude language of the arena) will catch you with your shield down!"

"Time enough between then and now," Hassim says, trying to catch my eye, but I turn away.

"Finish shaving; you don't want to prick her silken face with your whiskers."

That night he tries to give me a golden chain, which I thrust away, and he stares at me.

"A body'd think you were jealous. What is she but a way to get suckling pig instead of cutlets of old horse, and better wine than the swill they give us here? A way to freedom— yours as well, my Zad'ini," he says, trying to hug me close. I am not jealous but envious of what she can have from him. The lowest of whores is more free than I, who fear his loving touch worse than I fear the sword of any fighter.

Drought in the city; even in the training quarters and for us, the pampered pets of the city, there is scarcity and water is strictly rationed. The pool is changed only every tenth day in ad of every third; water for washing is in short supply. Beizun grumbles because she cannot wash her long splendid red hair every day with the scented soap an admirer sends; I, who have known real thirst, do not complain, because at least there is ample drinking water.

Prayers for rain are ʰ 'd ın all the public squares. I do not pray; I know nothing of their

gods and for me, prayer would be only a cha-
rade of conformity.

Then the Akharet decrees that all the gladiators shall attend a special sacrifice; Hassim
brings me this news, and tells me to put on my
finest garments, the richly colored scarlet silks
my patron sent me, and all the jewels I did not
sell. Thus decked out, I see my reflection in the
pool, and think to myself that I am barbarian—
and nevertheless beautiful.

While the procession is forming, Beizun
stands beside me, watching the men line up in
their fine clothes, Hassim is magnificent in sky-
blue brocades with twinkling jewels in his tur-
ban. Beizun has put away her battered armor
and wears a skirt and brief jacket of pure white
doeskin cut low across her superb breasts. Seeing
the pallor of her breasts, the long suntanned
legs bare to the thigh, I cannot imagine how
she can display herself so, outside the arena.
She only laughs at me and presses my fingers
against her heart, which I can feel beating under my hand, and I think of the arena and the
games which are coming within a tenday, rain
or no rain. And I think of the long-legged boy
who died in his first ten minutes in the arena,
and of how close I came to following him into
obscure death, and of how little it would take
to stop that heart beating under my hand, and I
am overcome with love and terror. And it could
be my hand which strikes.

The thought fills me with terror; she hears
my breath catch, and lifts my hands to her lips,

caressing the fingers gently. Before us, the bulls are led out for sacrifice, sleek and garlanded, full of life, pawing and stamping. The shaven-headed priests, clad only in kilts, sunburnt to the waist, circles of red on their naked pates, flash the long knives. One of the priests, muscled like a gladiator, steps forward and tosses a hoop of gilt as if at random; it falls over a ribboned horn, and at once two acolytes grab the horns and drag the animal forward. The bull thinks this is a new game, and tosses its head without seriously trying to escape; I watch the play as if it were a new gladiatorial contest, the bare-chested priests struggling, browned muscles springing into prominence as they drag the animal forward by force. The sacrificial priest raises his knife and as the others wrestle the horns forward and upward, so that the beast's throat is exposed, he makes a single long sweeping cut downward. There is a single long moan from the crowd, a curious sound of awe and satisfaction. Even I feel a curious pulling sensation in my gut as the knife flashes in the sun, blood spurts over the garlands and ribbons, and the sleek white sides of the animal are splattered with the same deep crimson as my dress. I hear Beizun give a little gasp of excitement and her hand, still clasping mine, tightens almost painfully.

The priest is kneeling over the fallen bull now, his white kilt bloodstained, digging inside; he wrenches at something red, holds it up dripping; the animal's heart. But I turn aside and vomit up everything I have eaten in the last three days.

Later I learn that this is an evil omen, that the sacrificial priest has sent to find out who spoiled the auspices of the sacrifice. Hassim tells them, "a newcomer to us and to the city; a barbarian girl from Gyre, and moreover, astray in her wits," so I escape punishment for spoiling the show.

I do not care if they think me witless. The sight sickens me; the waste of a living animal for some mummery of religion. The worst of it is that, later that day, the sky clouds over, and thunder darkens the arena; as we sit to dine (there is roast meat; the flesh of sacrificial animals is always sent to the tables of the Akharet and he in turn, I am told, always sends a great haunch roasted from the royal tables to grace the dinner of his gladiators). I join in toasting his generosity but have no taste for the roasted flesh, carved hot and dripping gravy like the crimson of the splattering blood. As Hassim lifts a dripping chunk to his mouth, thunder rumbles like earthquake, lightning streaks our faces, and sudden hailstones bounce into the open roof, rattle and fall; one strikes me on the head and I cry out more in surprise than pain, jumping up to run under the eaves, leaving my dinner of bread and fruit on the table.

One by one they follow my example, while the hailstones rattle and bounce until the courtyard is white with the ice-balls. Most of them are the size of my thumbnail, a few are as big as a baby's fist.

One strikes me, drawing blood from my forehead, and I fall, dizzied and half unconscious from the blow.

The next thing I know, Beizun is at my side, lifting me, and Hassim comes to try to shove her aside. They quarrel briefly about which will carry me to shelter. When Hassim lays me down in my usual sleeping place, kneeling at my side, I reassure him that I am not badly hurt, so he leaves me to Beizun to sponge my forehead clean of blood. She grimaces as he strides away.

"How possessive he is, your lover!"

"He is not my lover, but my friend," I tell her and she grimaces again, this time with frank skepticism.

"No? Who then?"

"I have no lover," I tell her, but I can see she does not believe me. I do not try to argue with her; let her think what she likes.

"If he is not yours, then, does it matter to you if I try Hassim? Or is one of the men here better at bedsport?"

"How do you think I would know?"

"You mean you have not tried them all yet?" she asks me. "I would have had them all, one by one! Or are they eunuchs here in the city?"

"I care not what they are," I tell her. "Any man that touches me—I kill! I am no harlot!"

Still I can see she does not believe me, so I turn away from her and let myself fall into sleep. In the night I wake with the silent men all sleeping round me, and in the moonlight through the slit windows I make out Hassim nearby on his pallet, and another dim form, long braids lying across his body; rising halfway to my knees I see Beizun curled up in the curve of his body, her head on his shoulder. I do not know what feeling it is that surges through me, but I am overcome with it, hardly knowing why the sight makes me smother painful weeping; I do not begrudge her Hassim's embraces, I tell myself I am glad for the pleasure shared by these two for whom I care so much.

Yet it is hours before I sleep again.

Morning; and by the poolside I am trying hard to knot up my long hair, enviously watching Beizun's flying fingers on her intricate braids. This is not the first time I have wondered; why do my hands not remember this simplest of women's skills, in the same way that my body remembered sword-strokes and shield-play? Beizun is conscious of my intent gaze, and breaks off to ask, "Want some help, Zadi?"

I let her take over the braiding, and remember the woman who combed my hair so gently that first morning out of the desert, before I was taken to the slave market; my first memory of gentleness; there are tears in my eyes as I feel her divide my hair for braiding, and I raise my hand to wipe them away. Beizun breaks off; "Am I hurting you?"

"Oh. No, no—" I tell her, my voice breaking,

and she listens in shock; but I do not want her to pity me, either. She says at last "So that is how you came here and how you lost your memory?"

"I wish I had lost less—or more," I say. "What I remember is what I would as soon not remember. Unless I died in the—the white fire and this is Hell."

Beizun grins, wryly.

"To tell the truth, kid, I've wondered. But I'm certainly alive, so I don't think that's what it is."

"Now you know how I came here," I say. "But I do not know how you came to the House of Fate. Were you kidnapped and sold as a slave, then?"

Her laughter is an unladylike guffaw.

"Kidnapped? Not a bit of it. I sold *myself* to the arena, my dear!"

"You sold yourself? But why?" I blurt out in shock.

"I have one weakness, and that is gambling," she tells me, "and I owed more than I could pay. The arena was better than any of the other alternatives; my creditors would have had me to a brothel in the copper mines. This is why I could feel for you. Better fight for a living than earn my bread on my back."

I join in a heartfelt "That's for certain!" but still I blink at her, remembering her curled up in Hassim's arms.

I wonder if she is reading my mind when she

says, "Are you angry with me because I slept with your lover?"

I could never be angry with her, and I tell her so. "I told you he was not my lover," I add, painfully. Beizun touches my cheek lightly, and says "He told me that he loves you very much, but that you don't love him at all. If he could have you he would never have touched me."

At this I cannot keep from crying again, and I feel her arms around me as I tell her—slowly, forced from me word by word—of my fear and failure. Her honest astonishment does more to unsettle me than anything yet.

"I can't even imagine what that would feel like—not even to want—" she breaks off, shaking her head. "I'd go crazy sleeping alone!"

"Maybe I am crazy, then." I have faced that before.

I am set to practice with her; she is taller than I and the Games-Master wants me to try the challenge of working against a greater reach. Day by day we work patiently, circling against one another; we are well matched, my greater maneuverability and quickness matching her strength and longer arms; usually she wears me out by longer stamina while early in the day I have the advantage because I move more quickly. Even in the training room our fellow gladiators stop to watch us, to shout encouragement at one or the other.

"Don't give such a good show with the red-head," Hassim says, as we square off for our daily practice. I am angry at his interference; the exhilaration of fighting with Beizun is pure pleasure. When I lifts my weapons against her, the thrill surges through me.

"So," he says, "do your own will, and be pitted against her in the arena; will it give you pleasure when the crowd yells for you to kill her?"

Ice surges through me; never once had I thought of that. Yet I know it is what the crowd would want most, of these two women they could not have, to stand by slavering while one spills the blood of the other, and I am sick at the thought, though one of us has wounded the other a dozen times, that we two might be pitted against the other for life or death. I want to shelter her in my arms, and when she slips and I inflict a small wound, I do not leap on her with joyous challenge, but burst into tears and weep, while she stares at me in dismay.

"What with you this morning, friend?"

I wail "I don't want to kill you!"

"You never will, this way," she says, makes a quick feint and I stumble, go down on the ground helpless; strange that somehow I have never guessed that she might wish to kill me in the ring to the roar of applause from the crowd. Somehow I have assumed that she feels for me the same as I for her. While I lie sobbing, too shaken to rise, she grabs me with rough kindness; "Did I really hurt you, Zadi'? Let's break off for the morning; I'm tired of all these bastards around slavering for blood from one of us!"

"Hassim says if we set up too good a show the crowd will be eager to see one of us die." Before what I have said penetrates, she flings back, with a great laugh and says, "Hassim is jealous."

"Mother-raping gods of Rhadamuth! The howling dogs in these crowds might be just that arrogant!" Her voice is suddenly gentle.

"Never, Zadieyek, I swear it." Then her eyes light with mischief. "We've got to get out of here. There's no time to waste. If we can't buy our way out—no time for that, we couldn't get the money within a year—we've got to escape. And I think I know how we're going to do it!"

She bends close and whispers her plan to me.

4 Those who have actually fought in the arena have the freedom of the City, I discover; I ask permission, readily given, to visit my patron.

She welcomes me with an embrace and a kiss; I am more aware of the meaning of this now. She offers me refreshment; iced fruits and a cool drink. I still have not learned to enjoy the overpowering taste of the wine, but I nibble at the fruits with real enjoyment.

"When are you to fight again?" she asks me, and I remind her of the special games only ten da:'s from now. "After today I will be training very hard," I tell her, not without guile, "and I will not see you again till after the games."

"I shall miss you," she says unprompted, and I realize that she has given me the opening Beizun told me how to recognize.

"Mistress—"

She interrupts. "Will you not call me Ifania?"

"Ifania, then. I was told you were seeking to build a *tammarim* of your own fighters—" and here I hesitate, but immediately she understands.

"Then we could be together as much as we wished," she says at once. "Would that please you, my beautiful one?"

Beizun has told me how to meet this, too.

"If we were always together, Ifania, you would grow tired of me. It is better as it is." And I pick up a peach and bite into its juicy, icy coldness, looking away from her.

"Never," she says. "But have you no friend or lover in the House of Fate, among the Akharet's fighters?"

"I have no lover," I say with conviction.

"And yet many of the men there are handsome and perfect—"

"I swear, lady, no man has touched me, or shall while I am whole and able to defend myself."

"Is this true?" she asks again, and again I reassure her.

"And it is possible for a woman to remain chaste while living among men?"

"For an ordinary woman, perhaps not; but I am a fighter and they know how well I can defend myself."

"I believe you," she says. "And what would you say if I told you I had chosen you for the first of my *tammarim* of fighters? The Akharet is a kinsman of mine; I am sure he would agree

to your sale. Shall I entreat him for permission
to purchase you from the House of Fate?"

I lower my eyes and murmur that the Lady
must do her own will.

"But would it make you happy to dwell in
my house, Zadieyek?" she asks me, now very
serious, her eyes seeking mine. I let her capture
my gaze for only a moment and then shyly
look away again.

"It would make me very happy," I murmur,
and she rises at once and claps her hands to
summon one of her house slaves.

"Send for my scribe," she demands, and when
the scribe, an old woman with many wrinkles,
comes in, she says to her, "Nurse, this is
Zadieyek, a gladiator of the House of Fate; she
will be joining our household."

The old woman sniffs scornfully. "Lady, you
have many devoted servants; what need have
you of a gladiator, a woman gladiator at that? If
you wish for a fighter, get yourself a proper
bodyguard, a man. . . ."

"No insolence, Nurse; you have urged me to
marry since my breasts were scarcely grown,"
says Ifania.

The old nurse grumbles at her, "And what of
that? If I am eager to see you with children in
your arms, is that a crime? Dearest Lady Ifania,
I have seen many of these infatuations of yours,
and the latest of them is this obsession with
fighting women. . . ."

Ifania stops her with an imperious gesture.
"Enough; bring your tablets and pens, and write

for me!" Grumbling, the old nurse fetches writing implements and ink and writes at Ifania's dictation to the Akharet, asking leave of her kinsman to buy "the female gladiator known only as Zadieyek." Then she turns to me:

"Is it true you have no other name? Or is it only that you do not wish it known in the arena? If you will entrust me with it, I swear I will never betray your confidence."

"I suppose that once I must have had another name," I tell her, "but whatever it may have been, I have no more memory of it then of what I may have been before birth or what I shall be after death."

"What do you remember first?"

"Fire," I say. "White fire blotting everything that might have been before."

"I have heard of such loss of memory," Ifania says. "My physician tells me it often comes from a blow on the head. Have you any memory of such?"

But try as I may, I remember only white fire shattering my world, and all the terror and abuse that followed. Ifania, seeing my look of distress, touches my hand gently. "There, there, I will not press you; but if you should remember, tell me. For now you shall be called what you will; Zadieyek, or otherwise as it pleases you, my dear."

I ask her "will you have a tammarim?"

"I had not thought of it," she says, "I want no brutes of fighting men about me, but it would please me to do what no noblewoman has ever done, and establish a full *tammarim* of woman gladiators. Are there any other women in the House of Fate who are full-fledged fighters?"

It was for this that I have been hoping, and I tell her about Beizun. "She is a woman of Rhadamuth who sold herself into the arena for gambling debts," I say.

"But is she beautiful? And is she truly like a woman? Some woman fighters have bulging muscles and are uglier than brutal men; if I have a *tammarim* of woman, I want them all to be possessed, not of skill at weapons alone but of such beauty that all the nobles in the city will envy me!"

"She is very beautiful," I say sincerely. "See her for yourself, Lady Ifania. And I have been told that we are well-matched for fighting."

"What is her weapon?"

"Like myself, she fights with sword and shield."

She bids the nurse and scribe to amend the letter, saying to the Akharet that she wishes to purchase the two female slaves who have not been chosen for the Akharet's own *tammarim*. She sends a trusted servant, one who is allowed to travel about the city—an old woman past the age where there would be any danger in walking even these streets alone.

"Now we shall see," says Ifania, and seats herself on a divan, patting the seat next to her as if inviting a kitten to curl up at her side. I join her there, and she takes my head in her lap, stroking my hair as if I were truly a pampered kitten. The old nurse glares, and I know that somehow I have made an enemy, here where I long to feel safe.

When the messenger returns, Ifania springs up to take the message. "Now we shall see," she says, and reads. The Akharet gives permission for my sale, but says that the female gladiator Beizun is as yet untried in the games and her worth unknown; he cannot as yet set a fair price on her.

Ifania shrugs. "So be it," she says. "It is Zadieyek I wanted anyhow; perhaps when Beizun has proven her worth he will be willing to sell." And she makes up a parcel of jewels and gold, the price set on me, and sends it off to the Akharet.

What have I done? I have exiled myself from the only home I know, the House of Fate, and cut myself off from the only two people in the world who mean anything to me—Hassim and Beizun.

I ask and receive permission from my new mistress to return to the House of Fate to collect my few possessions. She offers to send one of her servants instead and spare me the journey; but I wish to bid farewell to Hassim and Beizun, to tell them what has happened.

"I thank you, Lady Ifania, but truly I would rather go myself." And I suddenly know what to say. "I would rather not make enemies of your servants by sending them on my errands."

"If any of them show you unkindness, Zadieyek, tell me, and they will regret it."

Already I know she means this but I know the best way to win enmity would be to carry tales of this kind. I fasten on my sandals and set off through the streets of the Akharet's city, returning to the House of Fate, the nearest to a home that I have ever known. As I travel the streets I look at all the strangers who throng the city. Surely somewhere among all these varied specimens there must be somewhere men and women of my true homeland, somewhere in this babel of tongues I should hear the sound of my native language. But would I know it if I did or should I hear it as a stranger, unrecognized? I shiver at the thought and hurry through the streets.

"Zadieyek!" The doorman greets me. "I did not know you were abroad! Hassim was seeking you and he did not know either. I told him I had not seen you leave the House."

I go then in search of Hassim before I begin to gather together my small belongings: a few spare tunics, my weapons which are the most prized of my possessions. I find him in the garden by the fountain, where the Akharet's gladiators are permitted to walk in their free hours.

"Zadi—I could not find you," he almost reproaches me. "I was troubled for your safety."

I accept his affectionate hug as I would a brother's—but I know nothing of brotherly affection either.

Now I must tell him: "The Akharet has agreed to sell me to Lady Ifania, my patron."

"And you agreed to this, and would leave me, my Zad'yek?"

There is no way to soften it. I can only say with feigned coldness "Yes, I agreed to the sale." Defensively, "I am no man's property."

"Wrong, we all belong to the Akharet," he reminds me, then remembers: "But now you are free of that, property to a rich lady's fancy. Well, I wish you all happiness, Zadi'."

"We shall meet in the arena." I remind him, and he says with a shudder "All gods forbid we should meet so, Zadi'; it would grieve me more than I could possibly say, to be forced to kill you at the cost of my own life."

"I truly hope that choice will never be yours," is all I can think of to say to him, and fling my arms around him in farewell. "Hassim, don't be angry with me!"

He embraces me with great tenderness.

"Be happy, girl. Some day, maybe, we will be together again. Not here; somewhere far from here."

"May it be so," I say solemnly in farewell and run in search of Beizun to tell her the first part of our plan has succeeded.

"Ifania has purchased me from the Akharet, and tried to buy you as well, but the Akharet said your worth was unknown as yet. Perhaps after the next games ten days from now."

Beizun wants to know all that passed between us. I am too shy to speak of the Lady Ifani's caresses; but Beizun knows anyhow. "Soon you will be able to ask her for whatever you wish, while she is infatuated with you," she says shrewdly. "And when we are free of the Akharet's House, we will devise a plan to get us both free of the arena."

In Ifania's house it is difficult to train alone yet I dare not neglect it; the price of neglected training would be certain death beyond the Door of Fate, with Old Bloody's hand stern on my shoulder.

Ifania comes to watch me, asks if there is anything I wish for.

"An arms-master," I tell her, "I do not want to be killed when next I enter the arena."

"Yes, my dear, but I will find you a woman trainer, I will have no man around you." So she engages a weapons-master for me, a gnarled little woman past fifty, muscles like a black-smith, who has seen me in the arena and has much to say about my style of swordsmanship.

"That shield is too light for you; you must train with a heavier one," she tells me. "As it is now, your shield-arm and sword-arm are unequally developed." She points to a line of muscle on my shield-arm and gives me weights to practice with. She also drills me in somer-saults and cartwheels, at which Ifania protests—one of her amusements is to come and watch me train.

"She is not an acrobat nor a clown; leave her the dignity of a fighter, I beg you."

"Dignity be damned, unless it is your plea-sure to watch her die," says the little arms mistress, whose name is Marfa. "When she takes a fall in the arena, these acrobats' plays can save her life. And they are graceful in themselves, crowd-pleasers; they will find pleasure in seeing her somersault away from a danger rather than seem to run away." She turns to me and admonishes me: "Never, even in avoiding a blow, seem to flinch from it; these maneuvers make it appear you are deliberately seeking to please and amuse rather than dodging danger. If you always entertain the crowd you can cheat death much longer."

I am grateful for this new knowledge and practice faithfully. At the end of ever day I am bidden to dine with Ifania, and she seems to take pleasure in supplying everything I desire; though my new trainer has decreed that I am to eat even more sparsely than Hassim required. White meat of fowl, fish, a few green vegetables, and few sweets; even most fruits are denied to me.

Yet on the new regimen even in these few days I can feel my muscles more defined, my body firmer, stronger. Ifania treats me like a new toy, draping me in colorful tunics and hanging me with jewels. On the eve of the games, my trainer warns me to bed early with only a light meal: Lady Ifania sulks, because she has invited guests and wants to show off her new prize possession at the banquet.

"After the games; then you can display her as victor," says Marfa, and Ifania accepts the decree with a pout.

"If it must be, it must," she says, and herself takes me to the well-ventilated airy outdoor porch, screened against flies and dust, which she has placed at my exclusive service; herself undresses me and tucks me into my bed with the kiss of a little girl putting her doll to bed for the night. Indeed often Ifania seems to me like a child with a new doll, rather than a fighter's patron. She is not bloodthirsty enough for that.

Left alone—it is not far past sunset—I find myself almost unable to sleep, wondering what awaits me in the arena the next day. I have not been told; had I been in the House of Fate I would have known the schedule of the combats and perhaps seen my fated opponent. What if, after all, I am pitted against Beizun or even Hassim? Could I bring myself to kill either of them, even at the price of my own life? If I knew a God to pray to, I would offer up a prayer that this would never be demanded of me. I lie and toss and turn, remembering how before the last games Hassim had sought my bed and how I had not been able to give to him what he wanted of me—I, less free than any slave, helpless captive of old fears. I think of Hassim, remember Beizun curled up in his arms, and I truly hope that tonight she will comfort him when I cannot.

Obsessively, I replay every sword-stroke of my first fight against the net-fighter; will I be pitted tomorrow against net-fighter or another swordsman? Or swordswoman—even against

Beizun? I replay in my mind every sword-stroke we have ever exchanged.

A shadow falls across me and I hear a soft step at my side; it is Marfa.

"Not asleep? I would give you a sleeping-draught but it might slow your eye and hand for tomorrow," she says. "Afraid?"

To her I will not confess fear. "No, of course not."

"Pride is good," she says, "but you are not so stupid. Try to relax. Count down quietly; breathe deep." Her voice is soothing, lulling me, relaxing muscle by muscle till I am drowsy.

I am near sleep and Marfa has stolen away when I hear a softer step, a weight on the bed beside me. I hardly know whose arms wind round me, enfolding me close, a touch that both soothes and excites. Half asleep I think I am held again in Beizun's arms, that it is her soft breast I touch, held against her with great happiness. Murmurs of tenderness, touches which stir none of the revulsion I felt when men used me and I had no way to protest. More and more intimate the touches until at last a great joy overcomes me, and half waking, I know I am in Ifania's arms, held close and lovingly caressed. Her arms encircle me; on her warm breast I sleep, forgetting fear and the shadow of the House of Fate.

5 Sunlight wakes me early; I am still in Ifania's arms. Now I know what it is I have felt for Beizun and I am a little sad that it was not with her that first discovered this delight.

Yet I am glad to be well-loved by my mistress; and as I look at her she opens her eyes and greets me with a kiss. "It is early still," she whispers to me. "Soon I will send you my own bath-woman to bathe and dress you and make you beautiful for the arena."

This morning even the thought of the arena cannot lessen my confidence and happiness. Ifania slips away and after a time her bathing-woman comes to take me to the bath. She rubs my limbs with scented oils until my body is alive with energies I never knew; then clothes me in a new blue-green tunic Ifania has sent for me, and slips over my head the little crescent-moon amulet which was Ifania's first gift to me. Ifania comes to look me over before I am taken to the House of Fate to prepare for the games.

"You are even more beautiful than I knew, my Zadieyek," she says. "Be dreadful indeed to your opponents," and she encircles me in her arms with a kiss almost more tender than passionate.

"May I win for your glory, my dear mistress," I say to her, and she embraces me again.

"And for your own, loveliest one," she says, and puts a ring on my finger, carved from a crimson gem. I touch it to my lips and before I go she says, "Come back safe to me, my love." She has sent her own litter to carry me through the streets.

I am beginning to learn what it is to be the pampered favorite of a great lady. As the litter carriers bear me with their good-natured shouts of "Clear the way! A great one comes! Give way!" I hear the cries of approval from the crowds like the sea-roar from the spectators. I am carried to the door of the House of Fate beyond which no outsiders may come, and deposited among the fighters, clad in the colors of the Akharet's slaves and those of his consort. Hassim, clad in his finest, greets me with an air of amusement.

"How fine you are, my Zadi'! Your patron has clothed you in silks and scented you with the finest perfumes."

Then Beizun is at my side, smiling welcome. "Tell me, what is the schedule of the games? Do you know what I am to fight?"

Hassim says in great anger "I am a gladiator, not a butcher! Yet the Akharet—may he live forever," Hassim adds with such broad sarcasm that even I know he is wishing the Akharet in hell, "has decreed that today we are to fight against beasts. Beasts—to shame all his fighters!"

"What is wrong with that, Hassim?" I ask, "It seems to me it would be better to kill animals than to kill men."

"Think you so?" Hassim says scornfully. "There is neither art nor skill, nor honor to be gained in dispatching brutes who know not even why they are to die. If it pleasures the Akharet to see innocent beasts die, he has enough sacrificial priests who can convince him that it gives his Gods pleasure to see the innocent mangled; at least fighters know why they fight."

"If the Akharet takes pleasure in seeing men and women wounded and dying—" I begin hotly, but Beizun touches my shoulder.

"Silence, my Zadi. The very walls may have ears."

"Who questions the Akharet's will may end by dining on a mouthful of sand," Hassim reminds me. I forbear to remind him that he too has questioned.

The Master of the Games comes to announce the first of the combats.

Against a dozen wild bulls from the marshes

of Rhighun; Hassim and four other members of the Akharet's *fammarmim*.

Hassim may be scornful; but as I sneak a look at the bulls being driven in from the other entrance, I am terrified. The bulls are broad at the shoulders as water buffalo, and their eyes are fierce. Hassim picks up his long spear and signals to his fellow fighters. I can hear the cries from the attendants. One of the servants of the arena tells us that the gaming odds are. narrowed; the odds are four to five on the bulls to kill all five gladiators and two to one that the bulls will kill three of the five. Enraged, I wonder if Ifania has gambled on beasts against men.

The bulls charge, and Hassim with his long spear comes up to take the biggest and oldest of them in the flank. He drives in a spear with such force that a man would be down, but it serves only to infuriate the bull, who turns and charges; Hassim raises his sword and strikes in the neck. One bull is down, dying. The gamblers in the arena who have bet on the bulls to kill all five of the fighters scream with fury. Another of Hassim's fighters casts his spear but wounds the bull only in the neck and is charged, gored and tossed aside with an angry lift of the horns. A wet bloodstained rag flaps into a corner of the arena too late even for Hassim to save, though he goes in with a deadly accurate cast.

Two bulls lie dead on the arena sand; three more charge down in a wild tossing of horns, rough manes, and Hassim dispatches another quickly as any sacrificial priest. The noise of bellowing fills the arena; the smell of blood and dung. The bulls are easy to kill by a skilled fighter ... it is only tedious. I begin to share Hassim's outrage at this butcher's task and remember his words: nor art nor skill nor glory to be gained at this. One of his fighters lies dead at his side; a second, tripping on a loose sandal strap, loses his footing and goes down to be gored and flung aside. But only one of the great buffalo bulls remains; Hassim dispatches it with one quick stroke, and walks straight for the exit without even deigning to acknowledge the thunderous applause. The crowd does not like this; bad enough that he throws off their bets and loses them money, but he seems to scorn their praise. Next time he appears in the arena they will be out for his blood.

"Foolish," Beizun says, nervously testing her sword's edge on a fold of her tunic; it parts the silk like a feather. Now she is called into the arena against a monstrous tusker, a gray wrunkled beast with little half-blind eyes and a long trunk whose first charge sends her twisting to swing up on a railing, then plunge down to strike off the questing trunk with a single stroke of her sword. This sends the tusker into a blind frenzy, high eerier squealing as it plunges back and forth, seeking its tormenter; Beizun rises to thrust her sword through the eye and into the brain; the beast crashes down, its great weight shaking the arena like an earthquake. Within a few minutes she has dispatched it and is safely back behind the barricades. After this a fight between two net-fighters and a clawed lion; they swiftly entangle the lion in their net and spear it to death.

The crowd is angry. This is too easy; they want blood, the blood of men and women, not animal blood.

My name is called and with sinking heart I discover that I am to fight a great striped cat, four times my size; orange and white stripes cover it from tail to nose. Beizun whispers to me "Look at its eyes," as I pass her at the entrance.

The tiger smells the blood in the arena and stands snarling, pacing and lashing its tail. I note that the eyes are pale, blood pulsing in the iris; albino, half-blind in the daylight. I somer-sault past it, maneuvering so that as it lines up to charge the sun is full in the great cat's weak eyes. Still thirsting for blood, it charges and I cartwheel away, eager to give the crowd a show. At least some of them are shouting as I escape; they want to see me killed, no question about that.

I am not in a mood to oblige them despite the scream of delight as I go down under an incredibly fast swipe of a big paw, my arm pouring blood. My scarlet tunic will be ruined. The cat's swipe has tangled in the crescent amulet I wear and half stripped off my tunic so I stand near naked before them. I raise the sword over my head and bring it down, but it turns on the great cat's bone and I go down under the creature, hearing the crowd yelling for blood, swipe my sword up into the belly as its blood pours out over me. The weight of the cat crashes down, knocking me senseless, smothering me in its foul carnivore's breath. When the arena slaves come to haul the cat's body aside I crawl out alive, coming up into a row of cartwheels. There is applause, grudging perhaps, but nevertheless at least some people in the crowd are glad to see me alive. I hope my mistress Ifania is one of them.

As I return behind the scenes, Marfa is there, ready to scold me for the amulet which nearly cost me my life. "Never, never, twenty times never, wear jewelry into the arena," she storms. My silken tunic is bloodsoaked, no more than rags past wearing, and I stand all but naked before the fighters crowding into the backstage area. Marfa shoves me into the bathing pool, scolding one of the slaves into bringing me a fresh tunic. When I am covered decently again, Hassim comes to greet me, relieved that I am still alive; he had seen me fall beneath the tiger-cat and thought me finished. I am still in Hassim's arms when Ifania comes in search of me, having bribed her way past the gate guards. "I was so frightened," she tells me, throwing her arms round me, then over my shoulder sees Beizun in her white linen and long braids of copper fire.

"Your name and country?" she asks.

"I am Beizun of Rhadamuth," says she.

Ifania then demands, "I must have you; I am eager to have a *tammarim* of women."

At once Ifania sends again to the Akharet, with a bribe of jewels, and by the time she sends her litter to take us home, Beizun is her slave, the purchase contract sealed.

Rumor in the streets says the Akharet is angry; too many expensive beasts killed and the crowd disappointed because there has been so little blood shed. The mob too is howling for blood, thinking that the Akharet has shirked his obligation to amuse them.

"Barbarians," Beizun says with a sneer. We cuddle close together in the litter borne toward Ifania's house. "They care nothing for the skill we showed fighting; they only want to see blood shed and watch the deaths of men and women! How I despise them!"

"Yet you chose of free will to become a gladiator," I remind her.

"Do you know how long whores last in the copper mines, Zadi'? This is at least a slower death and less certain; there is some chance of escaping Old Bloody and buying free," she answers.

When we return to Ifania's house the bath-woman is waiting to bathe, massage and scent us, and give us fine fresh tunics and jewels. Thus arrayed we are bidden to Ifania's feast.

Our mistress's friends await us and I can sense the ripple of awareness and admiration as we come in, Beizun tall and elegant, her flaming hair radiant against her garment of white silk; I know that I too am beautiful, seeing my own darker hair and slenderer figure robed in azure, my dark eyes reflected in Beizun's eyes. Ifania too is beautiful, slender and prettily made in her patrician long gown. I had hardly realized how young she is, perhaps not yet twenty. "So what will you do with two beautiful fighting women, Ifania?" they ask her.

"Oh, I will think of something." She comes to show us to seats; furtively her hands seeks mind, a little touch to reassure herself. Beizun sees and suddenly I blush, remembering what Beizun said: "While she is still infatuated with you." And suddenly I feel a great pity for my mistress, knowing that in a very real sense she is at my mercy; I am slave and she is mistress but still all the power is mine. And I do not understand it or desire it.

This is the first time in memory that I have not been at the mercy of events: captive, prisoner, victim. When I seized the weapon and made myself gladiator rather than harlot, that was the first choice I had ever been able to make. Now I am aware that whatever happens from this moment will be what I cause to happen, and I am afraid, this is a frightening responsibility; not only to determine the course of my own life but Beizun's too, and even the life of my mistress Ifania.

There has been a queer little pause as if the world had stopped and then gone on again. Ifania still clings to my hand and I clasp my fingers around it. Why will she put herself in my hands that way? I still cannot understand.

"They are beautiful indeed," says the lady Evara, a friend of my lady, elegantly dressed but not half so beautiful as Ifania, her sandy hair thinned and graying, her long face traced with lines of petulance and self-indulgence. "So, Ifania, you have chosen to sponsor a *tammarim* of fighters? That is good; the Akharet grows old and lazy. That disgraceful exhibition of slaughter today—does he think he is running a butcher shop? And as for his consort—I was brought up with Clarmina, and she knows nothing of fighters and cares less. So you will give us proper games again?"

"I will try," Ifania answers, "but I know little of the arena. Perhaps these two can teach me. Tell me, Zadieyek, why would you rather fight men than beasts? That tiger came close to killing you today—is it more difficult to kill animals than men?"

I look around at the women, listening avidly to me, eager to know what it felt like to face death when none of them had ever felt the slightest danger. I am resentful; however I turn to my mistress.

"It is dangerous to fight animals because there is no way of knowing what they are thinking, or if they think at all," I answer slowly. "Men at least know what they are doing in the arena and why they are there. A dumb brute knows only that I am tormenting him and defends himself with his natural weapons; it is hard to kill a creature who has been attacked without reason, and knows not why he is being attacked."

"Why, the girl's an ethical philospher," says one of Ifania's friends scornfully.

"And it does not trouble your conscience to kill men who may have no more choice than the animals, being slaves sold to the arena?"

A knotty question that, and the woman asking it is not seriously interested in this point of conscience; she is making fun of me. Nevertheless I take the question seriously, glad to have a chance to think and express myself about these things.

"No, it troubles my conscience not at all, Lady," I say to her seriously. "I have chosen to fight rather than to die; a man I fight has made that choice also or he would not have come to the arena at all."

Ifania says vehemently, "You will fight no more brute beasts, that I promise you, Zadieyek. And you, Beizun, what think you of fighting animals?"

Beizun laughs. "They are too easy to kill," she says, "because I know what I am doing and they do not. There is no room in such contests for skill or even strength. I am in the arena to display skill and win fame; but as a fighter, not a butcher's apprentice! If I had faced a swordsman today and won against him with my skills, tonight I should be proud. But what is there to be proud of—that I managed to invent a way to torture a big stupid beast to death?"

"Proud that it was not you lying dead," said one of the women, and Beizun shakes her coppery mane.

"Glad I am not dead, indeed; but not *proud*, Lady. I take no pride in such slaughter. I am willing to pit my skills against intelligence aimed to kill me; here it was simply the brute skill to keep out from under the big tusker's feet until I figured out his vulnerable points. If I had had to kill the creature to feed some starving folk, then perhaps it would be a matter for pride, to do what I set out to do. To stalk it and hunt it down in its native jungles where it had a chance to evade me, perhaps. But not to have it driven into an unfamiliar space with no place to hide, so that all I needed to do was drive my sword and spear home. No, Lady, that is neither the skill of the fighter or even of the hunter, but only of the slaughterhouse. If I wished to learn butchery, I would have apprenticed myself to a butcher."

"Then, since you must be a fighter, will you welcome properly arranged games?" asks Ifania's friend.

Beizun replies, "I will. I fear no man with sword or shield. This is the life I have chosen. I have been a warrior since I was tall enough to grasp a sword-hilt."

"And you like the life?" asks another woman. "You chose the world of a warrior? It was your free will, not a forced choice? You were not born to it?"

"I was not. My father was a merchant and he would have had me grow up to be a house mouse, to marry young and wear fine clothes, to paint my face and lie with one man, and bear him many replicas of his ugliness," said Beizun. "When I became a mercenary soldier, he drove me from his house in the shift I wore and no more."

Ifania looks from Beizun to me and says slowly, "I can understand your choice, Zad-ieyek—you were sold to the arena and had no choice save fighting or harlotry, and I might have chosen as you did rather than being given over to be used by men. But you, Beizun, there were other suitable choices for you. Why did you wish to be a warrior?"

Beizun shrugs and says, "It seemed at the time that it was my only choice. Why does anyone choose as they choose?" I can tell that she is angry with this inquisition. Yet I too would like to ask her that question and hear her real answer some day.

Even Ifania senses her anger, and says, "But come, the banquet grows cold while we ask questions," and signals to the servants to put food on the table. "Tonight we will forget the trainers and you shall eat whatever you wish." She helps me herself to several dishes she knows I like, urges Beizun to choose her own delica-cies, pours wine.

When we have all eaten and drunk till we can hold no more, Ifania tells us her plan.

"I will have a *tammarim* of the most beauti-ful fighters ever seen in the arena," she says. "Then will I show the Akharet what proper games should be." But Evara mocks at her.

"Where will you find them? In all the city I think there are only these two."

"There is Marfa, their trainer," Ifania says. "Perhaps she would make a third, or knows of a third. Then I will send these two to find others, recruit and train them to the arena."

"And where will you send?" Evara asks.

"Wherever I must. Even to Gyre if need be; if Gyre produced Zadieyek, I have no doubt there are other fighting women who could be induced to come and exhibit their skills!" Ifania says. "If there are two women who will choose the warrior's life, there must be others."

I drop my fork and stare at Ifania in astonishment and dismay. I wish to be free of the arena, not seduce others into it. But her friends all join in with excitement at the thought that women fighters might come to dominate the arena. I do not know why the thought pleases them so much. What, I wonder, in the name of any or all of the Gods, excites them in the idea of women fighting in the arena? Do they not know that I would change my life with any of them? Do they think I chose this life because I liked it? I look at Beizun and discover that she is smiling; evidently the thought pleases her too. I wish we could get away from these rich women and their new amusement, and talk sanely together. I really would like to know why Beizun has chosen this life when not compelled; I can understand that she chose it in preference to the brothels of the copper mines, when gambling debts made that imperative; but why had she chosen to become a mercenary soldier in the first place?

The evening is endless; but at last, as all things must, it drags to a close and I am free to seek rest. I wonder if once again Ifania will command my presence or seek me out. I have drunk far too much of the sweet wine, and I stagger as I turn my steps toward the airy porch where I sleep; Beizun comes to put her arms round me and steady my steps.

I have remembered something else, while I watched Ifania writing to the Akharet, and I confide it to Beizun.

"When I saw our mistress, Lady Ifania, making up her parcel of bribes, I saw myself writing—reading too."

She scowls at me. "You are drunk, Zadi'. Hush."

I am angry because she does not believe me and I insist in a louder voice, "I can read too, and write; give me a pen and I will show you."

Now she lowers her voice and hisses in my ear, enraged.

"Shut your foolish mouth or you will have us both to the torturers! Don't you know that the penalty for teaching a slave to read or write is a hundred gold *decars* and the penalty for the slave found doing either is to lose a hand? Sometimes they cut it off one finger at a time— and sometimes worse; you don't want to know."

I feel a flood of—no, not fear—anger and disgust. How barbarous these people must be; more than ever I am relieved that I am not one of them! The righteous rage is replaced by bewilderment; if I am not one of them, what am I then? One thing is sure, I come from a people who take it for granted that reading, and writing too, are—I fumble for concepts—simple rights, where every child is instructed in these things as a matter of course.

When I say this, Beizun scoffs. "Even slaves?"

I try to remember and suggest: "I don't believe there are slaves among us."

"Fantasy," Beizun scoffs, "How would any work get done?" and I know I have overtaxed her credulity and she will hear no more.

Yet as I crawl into my bed, and Beizun, as yet having been assigned no place of her own to sleep, curls up beside me, I search my memory for more scraps of that curious sureness, when I was relieved that these people were alien to me, barbarians, savages. But there is no more to the memory and I remember the only time I had any feeling like it; at the first feast in the House of Fate, after my first fight in the arena; given a carved wing from a roast bird, and my first hunger satisfied with a few bites of the rich fatty meat and crisp skin, I flex it, noting the tendons still attached to the bones and the strangeness of the wing; it seems to me that it should be a different shape, the bone hollow—how does a creature this size manage to fly? Maybe it doesn't, I think, suddenly remembering flightless birds raised only for food. But try as I may, I can force memory back only to the white fire dividing my life, and these glimpses from any tenuous *before* are brief and fleeting.

Beizun pulls me into her arms, but the wine still fuzzes my mind, and I am too listless to respond to her gentle touches; my head flops back and I whimper and snore. But I am pleased to curl up in her arms; held securely there, I know the old nightmare will not touch me, the dream in which again, endlessly, I cross the desert tied to the back of some animal, and whenever I am untied and left loose, there are men to come and fumble at me, an endless nightmare of violation and thirst.

Once indeed I waken, feeling hands drawing aside my gown and touching me, with a gentleness in which there is neither pain nor dread; I half waken and discover my mistress Ifania's hands on me, seeking and enticing; I am still too sleepy and drunk to respond, and at last, sighing with frustration, she turns aside and draws Beizun into her arms; but I am not afraid either, and I fall heavily asleep again without dreams.

When the sunlight wakens me, Ifania lies between us, an arm round each, and when her old Nurse comes in search of her, she begins to scold.

"A pretty sight for Your Dignity, indeed," she storms. "And if you intend to have a *tammarim* of these, must we seek through the marketplace for a bigger bed?"

Over Ifania's turned head Beizun meets my eyes with a mirthful twist of her face and I dive into the bedclothes to smother childish giggles.

Ifania strives for dignity indeed: "Be off with

you, Nurse, it is nothing to you where or with whom I spend my nights? Go and prepare my bath and send the bath-woman to us."

"At once, Lady; but it is not my business to wait on these unladylike hoydens! *Female gladiators*, my lady! Have you no thought for the reputation of your lady mother and your noble father if you have none for your own? What will it be next—dancers? Acrobats from some traveling circus?"

"Have done, Nurse; it is for certain that the city will gossip about me and mine, however I choose to spend my time; even should I spend all my days blamelessly arranging flowers for the Akharet's court receptions, they would find some scandal to speak," Ifania commands. The Nurse grumbles herself away at last, and Ifania lays her hand on my shoulder and pulls me out from under the sheet, half stifled.

"Are you laughing at me, Zadieyek?"

"Oh, no, never," I insist.

"You must not mind old Hatara," Ifania says, bending over to kiss my cheek. "She nursed my mother before me, and such old family servants have privileges, even here. She speaks her mind, but she is good-hearted and never really unkind to anyone."

I can think of nothing to say, but Beizun as always knows the proper courteous phrases.

"If she is loyal to you, Lady Ifania, then Zadieyek and I will be loyal to her as well; who is cherished by our dear mistress is dear to us as well, is she not, Zadi'?"

I manage to say, "Truly so, Lady," and Ifania rises as the bath-woman comes through the door.

"When I have finished my bath I will send her to dress you," she says. "I will have an errand for you both, later. Today I begin my search for fighters for my *tammarim*."

Alone Beizun grins at me in delight.

"Freedom, Zadi'. We will soon have the freedom of the city, and I will bet all the profits of my next fight that before the moon wanes we will have more than that."

I do not share her optimism. Suddenly it has crashed in on me that, however petted and pampered and trusted, we are still slaves, and our very lives and deaths depend on the fickle will of a neurotic girl with a new toy. The prospect seems to me appalling.

But nothing happens that day; Beizun and I are bathed, massaged, dressed and perfumed; but when we rejoin our mistress, she says only that since yesterday was taxing, we may spend the day at ease. Marfa comes to insist that we spend at least an hour or two in exercise to loosen our muscles. "Otherwise," she insists, "you will be too sore to walk across the room tomorrow."

She also tends the half-forgotten scrape across my arm from the giant cat's claws. "The claws of a carnivore bear poison," she tells me. "You could take poison in your blood and lose the arm."

I had not known this and I am grateful to the old warrior, knowing that she, at least, is a friend. When I pick up my sword to work with Beizun, my arm is almost too sore to lift, and I groan, unwilling to start. I would rather rest till the ache vanishes, but she insists: "No, no, no; after an hour of exercise you will feel much better."

I grumble, but I obey, and much to my surprise after only a few minutes of exercise my limberness comes back and I astonish Beizun with a row of cartwheels across the floor.

"Where did you learn that?" she demands. I point to the old woman, and Beizun demands, "Can you teach me too, old lady?"

"You do not need it," Marfa says bluntly. "They will look at you no matter what, particularly when you dress like that. Zadi' is small, thin—she needs some crowd-pleaser like that."

Beizun guffaws loudly. "But maybe I would rather show off my skill than my tits," she says to Marfa, and I promise, "Never mind, Beizun, if she won't teach you, I will."

We spend much of the rest of the afternoon practicing somersaults and clever flips and backbends. Beizun proves to have a talent for it, and with her long legs and loose copper hair she is at once far more spectacular than I. I take pleasure in watching her, and the time speeds by without noticing until the old Nurse, Hatara, comes to warn us that the mistress has returned and will expect us to dine with her.

At table I notice it is training diet again, baked white fish served with greens and thin slices of melon. There are pastries and wine for Ifania, but I am touched that she waves them away, choosing to share our diet.

Hatara nags, "My lady, you must eat to keep up your strength," but Ifania says, "If two fighters can keep their strength up on such a diet it cannot harm me," and sends away the wine and sweets.

Later she summons Beizun to her side. "Have you traveled widely in the kingdom?" she asks, and Beizun gives a brief resumé of her travels, which I hardly believe, though I learn later that, far from exaggerating, she has given only a modest and partial list of all the places where, as a mercenary, she has fought or traveled.

"This is my plan," said Ifania, "for three days you shall travel around the city here, trying to search out women fighters for my service; and when those days are gone, I shall send the two of you traveling in other cities and kingdoms, to seek more women who will fight in my name in the arena. Is that agreeable to you?"

I hardly know what to say, being genuinely reluctant to leave this first person who has shown me kindness. But Beizun as always has the properly tactful thing to say.

"It will grieve us to leave you, kindest of mistresses, but if this is your desire, it will be our greatest pleasure to do your will."

Since this is exactly how I feel, I have no hesitation in repeating and seconding what she says. I feel myself eager to do whatever Ifania wishes of me. Yet too often I have the feeling that Beizun is subtly making fun of our mistress. The next morning Ifania has her scribe write out for us passes that will allow us to travel freely anywhere in the city.

I ask Beizun as we leave Ifania's mansion and turn into the next street, "Where shall we go first?" I have no idea where I would go to find women fighters.

"We will begin," Beizun says, "with the schools of martial arts, and ask if there are any women pupils. Some men will not train women in such arts."

"Why not?"

"For the same reason that many masters will not risk the penalties of teaching a slave to read or write: all too many men know that their women have so much reason to hate them that if they were taught to fight, or to kill, they would turn their new skills first on their masters. In fact, some men clamor for laws making it illegal to teach women the arts of fighting; but so far, no such laws have been passed—not in this city at least. Give them time."

I do not understand; I suppose if I had all my memories I might know what Beizun is talking about.

Beizun goes into a wineshop and inquires about the schools of martial arts in the city.

"A school in martial arts which accepts women as pupils?" asks the tavern-keeper with a guffaw. "You want to study fighting, dearie? What for? You don't need to learn to beat men up, surely; I'll give you a bed and board and all you'll have to do to earn it is to wait on my customers in that little leather apron."

Beizun grabs him by a handful of his tunic front and drags him close.

"That's why," she says and already her knife is at his throat. "To guard against pricks like you with offers like this. Look, friend citizen, I asked you a civil question; answer it or say you don't know, but I've better things to do than fend off indecent propositions. I'm a working girl and my patience is short."

The tavern-keeper exhales beery despair.

"No offense meant, young woman. Sorry. No harm in asking, I thought. Schools of fighters? There's one in the next square past the fountain, big house with two red pillars in front. Run by a woman, I heard. She can tell you all she wants to about the others, better'n I could. Let me go, you're choking me."

Beizun pitches him handily into a corner; he picks himself up slowly, with a wary glance at her still-unsheathed knife. As he sidles past her, with a lecherous look at her long legs, she half turns and gesturers with the knife.

"Don't even think about it," she warns, "or you'll be sending out invitations to a castration party: yer own. Hands to yerself, now."

"Oh, for sure, lady," he says ingratiatingly. "Do put the knife up, now, there's a nice girl. Can I offer you and your companion a beer? On the house," he adds, and since I am hot and thirsty from the dust in the streets, I make a grateful gesture, but Beizun says curtly, "Can't. We're in training. Thanks anyhow," and spins on her heel to go.

The house in the next square by the fountain is farther than he had led us to believe, and by the time we sight the two red pillars, I am exhausted from walking in the dusty glare of the sun. There is a huge knocker in the form of the head of a goat; Beizun pulls the goat's beard and inside the house we hear a faint and far-off chime.

After a bit the door opens and a woman stands before us; half naked, wearing only a tiny white loincloth. She is virtually breastless, barefoot, with muscles like old Marfa's. The sight of her immediately convinces me that we have found the right house, as do her sharp words. "If you have come for lessons, my classes are full until Solstice; I may have a few vacancies then."

"I have no need of lessons," Beizun says. "I have business to discuss which could be to your advantage and the advantage of some of your pupils, if you wish them well."

"Come in, ladies," says the little woman. She is fair-skinned, fair-haired, with freckles scattered across her nose. "My name is Cleodora. May I offer you a cooling drink?"

Gratefully we follow her into an atrium with grapevines growing across trellises for shade; she offers us chilled fruit juice, and across the courtyard, on a patch of soft sand, we see a number of young girls practicing with wooden sticks which clatter and echo in the silence.

"May I know your names?" Cleodora asks us.

"I am Beizun of Rhadamuth—"

"I knew I had seen you somewhere!" Cleodora exclaims. "I am not a regular follower of the arena, but did you not fight a great tusked beast at the Akharet's games?"

"I do not brag of it, Lady Cleodora; I am a fighter in the House of Fate, and I do not choose my own combats. I would prefer to fight against strong men," Beizun answers.

"Are you a member of the Akharet's tammarim?"

"I am not; my mistress is named Ifania," Beizun tells her. "And she has a fancy to own a *tammarim* of woman fighters. Do you know of any who are for sale?"

"I do not," says Cleodora. "I instruct only free women; there are no slaves among my pupils." After a moment she says, "Would you truly seek to lead other women into such slavery?"

"There are worse slaveries," Beizun says, and after a moment Cleodora nods.

"I can well imagine; I was not condemning your choice, Beizun of Rhadamuth. For all that, it is not my choice, nor would it be the choice of any free woman, I think."

"Nor can I condemn you for your refusal," Beizun says. "Yet, should you hear of any woman fighter seeking a good situation—"

"And poor enough to have no other choice, I understand you well," says Cleodora.

We thank her for the cold drinks and take our departure. As we come out again into the sunlight, I notice a slight figure following us. I whisper about it to Beizun and she steps around the corner, turns back to seize the wrist of our follower. There is a little squeak of dismay and I see that she has gripped a slender girl not more than fourteen years old, with her hair in a long braid and a knee-length tunic.

"What do you want with us?" Beizun growls.

"Oh, please, I heard you say you were seeking fighters . . . and I have heard that even slave fighters can grow rich—if they live," says the girl. "I have an old mother and my brother who should have helped me care for her is crippled in both his feet. How could I become a fighter?"

I say quickly, "First you must grow up, my dear; the arena is no place for children."

"I am no child," she cries indignantly, "I have been a woman now for more than a year!"

"Are you one of Cleodora's pupils?" Beizun asks her, and she replies, "Yes. I would rather fight than keep house, and I think I have more talent for it."

"You think you can fight?"

"I know I can," the little girl says proudly. "Try me."

Beizun draws her sword and slowly circles; the child rushes forward, her stick between her hands, and in a moment, Beizun's sword goes flying through the air and the girl rushes in, cracking her stick down on Biezen's head till she staggers.

"You see?" she said pridefully.

"You took me off guard," Beizun grumbles. "Shall we take her to Ifania?"

I think she is exactly what Ifania is looking for. But I do not know if free women are allowed to fight in the arena. Free men may be fighters—so Hassim once told me—but I do not know if the law covers free women.

I suppose Ifania will know. "What is your name, my dear?" I ask her.

"Aris," she tells me, picking up her fighting-stick. I notice it has been polished and varnished to high gloss, and that the slippers she wears are of whitened leather.

"Aris, why do you think you want to fight in the arena?" I ask her.

"For money," she tells me. My mother is old and sick and my brother crippled. My father died when I was only a baby."

"You will find it quite a different matter—fighting in deadly earnest in the arena, with sharp weapons, from fighting your playmates with little sticks," Beizun warns her.

The girl replies seriously "I know that. But if I am conquered, I can only die once. My brother wants me to marry an old rich man. I should die a thousand times over, shut up in his house. Better to keep my pride, fight cleanly in the arena, and die a virgin."

"And if you die, who will care for your mother?"

"A friend of my father's has offered to marry her, but she has said she will not marry while her marriageable daugher is still unwed. She thinks it best for me to marry," Aris says.

Beizun replies, "Have you considered that your mother may be right?"

"Often," Aris says, "but I cannot convince myself."

I wonder while Beizun questions her; *Does anything but desperation drive a woman to the arena?* Not, I think, in this city, though in Rhadamuth, where Beizun has told me that many women become soldiers and mercenaries, or in Gyre where warrior women (I myself?) are ordinary, perhaps it is different.

"Tell me, Aris, what will you do if we refuse you?"

"I will cut my hair and steal a set of my brother's clothes, and make my way across the desert to Gyre, where a woman may be a warrior," Aris says, and Beizun, with a sigh, capitulates.

"Come along, then. Do you think Ifania will like her, Zadi?"

I am all too sure that she will.

When we reach home and Aris tells her story to Ifania, Ifania is appalled.

"Aris, are you not the daughter of Zyphun the silk merchant?" she asks, and Aris admits it, though Zyphun has been dead many years.

"There will be trouble if I take a free woman into my house to train her for the arena," she says. "What says Marfa? Can you train her so she will survive in the arena?"

"I am near to fifteen," says Aris, "when a citizen is fifteen years old, she may enter legally into a contract, even to fight in the arena."

Ifania shrugs. "Be it as you will; now I have four fighters toward a tammarim," she says. "But send word to Cleodora and to your mother. I do not want to face a charge of kidnapping a citizen's freeborn daughter."

7 Three days after Aris comes to us, we leave the city, Beizun and I, and a bodyguard hired by our mistress, three huge men, trained fighters.

Beizun is angry and indignant. "I need no men for bodyguard," she says to Ifania at that final breakfast. "Do you truly think I cannot care for myself against any man?"

"But for traveling beyond the borders of the city, in the desert, where no women go? You would be prey for the first caravan of slavers to encounter you," Ifania says. "You travel with the bodyguard, Beizun, or you do not step beyond this courtyard. No, it is no use trying to cajole me, my mind is made up."

Beizun shrugs and subsides; better to travel with a bodyguard than not to travel at all, and it occurs to me that perhaps Ifania suspects our half-formed plan to escape. The bodyguards may be guarding Ifania's interest in valuable property. And this creates sudden surging resentment; kindly though Ifania is to me, I feel, deep down at gut level, that no man or woman should own another like a cane or a set of old clothes to be bought and sold. Yet here slavery is taken for granted, just part of the system. I do not understand from where these alien thoughts come; the faraway and mysterious land of Gyre, perhaps? My unknown homeland?

Ifania's house is in an uproar with our plans for departure, everyone running upstairs and down for one thing and another we might need. Waterskins, tied on the backs of the great desert-going beasts; tents for the nights spent in the desert; stores of food, bread and fruits and dried meats. And at last Ifania gives to Beizun the most precious thing of all, a written pass stating—I cast my eyes over it without letting Ifania see that I can read it—that her servants Zaideyek and Beizun are free to travel where they will in search of women for her *tammarim*, and that no one shall interfere with the lawful property of Ifania, daughter of Ilfanios.

Property. I am nothing more than property; yet that statement protects me.

Aris comes down and flings her arms around me in farewell.

"Why can't I go with them, Lady Ifania? I could protect them; I am a fighter," she says.

Ifania gently embraces the girl and says, "You are too young; a maiden your age would be seized and stolen, almost before she left the city."

"But I am a free woman, a citizen's daughter," Aris protests.

"And how would you prove it, in places where no man knew your father's name or your mother's?" Ifania counters. "No, Aris, stay within the walls of my house where you are safe." And Aris sulkily subsides, while Marfa tried to pacify her by telling her of the sword being made for her and the new armor.

I am just as well pleased that Aris is to be left behind. The thought of traveling free excites me, I know not why—to see what lies behind strange horizons, the need to know other places and see the strange customs of other people—it fills me with excitement, not unmixed with fear—but rather than paralyzing me like other fear, this fear seems both a tonic and a stimulant. I know I am doing what I should be doing, and for the first time I can remember I am content.

Yet beyond and through all this, I look at Beizun and something within me is filled with excitement of quite another kind at the thought of many nights alone on the trail.

A final embrace from Ifania. "Are you glad then to be leaving me, my Zadi'yek?" she asks in tender reproach, and I say to her, "Not glad to be leaving you; no, my mistress, never that."

And in some curious fashion it is true. In this house I have known the first sustained kindness of my life, the first sense of being valued for anything other than my skill with sword and shield; here I do not need literally to fight for the right to live. I know that one part of Ifania's interest in me is in my skill, but that she would love me and continue to treat me with tenderness even should I refuse to fight; in fact, it occurs to me that if I should beg her to free me of the arena she would do so, and would still care for and cosset me. But then I would still be a kind of harlot, and the thought puzzles and annoys me. Is there no other choice for a woman without riches? I remember that Aris chose the sword as a way to avoid being sold to a man who wanted her, even though he called it marriage instead of harlotry. I find it hard at this moment to understand the distinction.

A final embrace from our mistress for Beizun, a pat on the back from Marfa for each of us; and we climb into the saddles of the riding beasts and they step out slowly, with plaintive cries of protest. The swaying motion makes me ill, and I try hard to focus my eyes and steady myself to the movement of the swaying saddle beneath me. Quickly I gain control. Beizun is leading; I ride after her, then our three hulking bodyguards, and there is another beast laden with our tents and supplies. We form a formidable caravan, where, I confess to myself, two women alone riding through the desert would be too much like a temptation to the lawless men who live in the wild spaces.

We move at the beasts' deliberate pace along

the cobbled streets, swaying with the rhythm of their step, smelling dust. A chilly and erratic breeze sways the little bells on their harnesses into curious melody. After a time I see that the clouds have come together in the sky to obscure the sun, and big cold drops of rain begin to fall. I hear Beizun cursing under her breath and I drop back to ask what is the matter.

"I should have known the rainy season was near," she says, "but I thought we would have a few days still before it began."

"The rainy season?" I do not remember. "You mean it will go on raining like this?"

"For the next three moons." Beizun tells me, "Oh, not every day of course, but more often than not."

"In the desert too?"

"Oh, no. Once we are all the way into the desert, probably it will be all dry and hot. But the desert is a long way from here." She looks intently at me. "I thought you crossed the desert coming here."

"I did." But it seems to me that we went directly from the desert to this city; is there more time lost from my memory?

We ride through the rain, pulling thick rugs over our heads; but the damp surrounds us, and the chill sends gloom all through my mind and heart. Toward evening a hole in the clouds reveals the setting sun through the rain, and the distant watery sun raises my spirits. The city is far behind us; we are riding on a well-bricked road, between high aisles of trees, bending and coming together over our heads.

The sun vanishes and almost at once a chilly twilight all but blinds us. Far in the distance some little twinkling lights betray a house or a town—I cannot guess which, but the biggest and most ruffianly looking of our bodyguards seems to know where we are going.

"We will lodge for the night at the inn of Dargan," he tells Beizun when she turns to question him. Soon, as the night darkens more deeply round us, we are riding through the gates of a walled enclosure.

"The inn," says our bodyguard. I am stiff with riding, and glad to be helped down from my beast, to walk about a little in the courtyard with straw underfoot. A little fat man hobbles out from the main building, and calls out to the bodyguard.

"Alban! Welcome, cousin," he says and I see a glance pass between them that chills me. This rascal bodyguard Alban and the innkeeper Dargan are well known to one another. I whisper to Beizun that we are in danger, we must not for a moment lower our guard: I do not trust the guard for a moment, and now I know I must not trust the innkeeper either.

"So near to Jemmok," Beizun says, disbelieving. "Surely fear of the Akharet's wrath would deter them from any mischief this near the city!"

Inside the inn swords, shields, spears hang on the wall. The fat innkeeper waddles over to offer us beer, and I sip at it, disliking the bitterness; but Beizun drinks with pleasure.

I ask the innkeeper, "What are the weapons?"

"Mementoes of my days in the arena," he says. "For five years I was in the *tammarim* of the Akharet's consort, and that great axe—" he points to it, his eyes glowing—"is the weapon I bore in my last fight, which freed me of the arena; my patron bought me free, and set me up in this inn."

"I too am a swordsman of the House of Fate," I tell him, "and Beizun as well."

"Truly?" He turns to Alban. "Ye did not tell me this, you dog!"

I turn to see Beizun slumped in her chair, sleeping heavily.

"Never fear," Dargan says, "a harmless sleeping draught. But I'll have none from the arena betrayed in my house!"

My hand is already on my sword.

Alban stammers, "I did not know; they are slaves of the Lady Ifania—" and cringes away. Now I know he has already betrayed us, I am ready to kill, but Dargan stands between us, protecting me from Alban, and Alban no less from me.

"They would sell for a good price in Lafhaain," says Alban pleading, but Dargan is obdurate, stepping between us, forcing my sword down.

"I fought in the arena, and any fighter from the House of Fate is my sister and my brother," he says. "Tell me, girl, what did you fight in the last game?"

"An albino tiger-cat," I tell him, and he nods.

"I heard of that fight," he says. "Tell me, does Hassim of Lerfaugh still fight?"

"Hassim? He is my friend, he befriended me when first I was sold to the House of Fate," and Dargan flings his arms around me, and overturns the pot of drugged beer into the straw.

"Bring the best wine from the cellar," he calls, and when a servant brings it, he pours for me. "Now tell me, girl, when did you come to the House of Fate? I remember my first fight there—the axe was my weapon. And Hassim and I fought and I came close to killing him; afterward we became friends—"

So Hassim knew what he spoke of when he warned me against being too well matched with Beizun. It is the beginning of a long night of stories about the arena. The air is thinning for dawn, and Beizun stirring, when I drop off to sleep, exhausted, to wake near sunset to a sound of rain on the roof, and Beizun at my side.

"We have lost a whole day," she says. "Did you sit up all night telling stories of the arena with Dargan? He has guarded you all day—and he drove that wretch Alban forth from here—he wouldn't let me kill him, but he swore on his life that no one should harm us under this roof while he had breath."

Our belongings are packed up for departure, and Dargan asks Beizun: "What of these other bodyguards; can you trust them?"

"I know nothing about them," Beizun says, "Lady Ifania chose them; I have no reason to think they are not honest men eager to earn their hire."

"Nevertheless I do not trust them," I say, and Beizun and I decide we will keep careful watch over our supposed "bodyguards"—we will know whose bodies they are guarding, and why.

It is raining again, a dismal drizzle, when we set forth from Dargan's inn. Even so I prefer it to the blazing heat and thirst of the desert, but Beizun is as cross as a wet cat, and we ride side by side without speaking, wrapped in dreary silence. That night we camp and set up our pavilions in the rain, eating only some bread and dried fruit, and go to rest with our bodyguards outside the tent; Beizun falls asleep in my arms at last but I stay awake for hours, afraid of attack, until finally I sleep, exhausted, and wake safe and unharmed. Even so I am not overly inclined to trust them, but will wait till I have reason for suspicion.

This begins a pattern of days of travel where we ride till we are exhausted and saddlesore and seasick from the motion of our beasts; camping at night in the dampness (for the rainy season is now fully under way) till every garment we own bears a thin white spidery coating of damp mold, and everything we eat tastes faintly of it. I sleep cold, and dream at night of fire and warmth. Even the warmth of Beizun's body in the night cannot warm my cold feet.

After ten days of this the sun comes out, and we stop on the trail to spread out clothing out to dry, tell the first of our bodyguards to spread out our bread to dry so it will perhaps lose that all-pervasive moldly smell.

"Perhaps in the next town we can buy fresh-baked bread," Beizun suggests.

"There is a great bazaar in the next town," the bodyguard answers. "It is the gateway to the desert."

Perhaps, I think, *there we will find some fighting women.* I suggest, this to Beizun and she says, "Perhaps. But we are not likely to find many women warriors until we reach Rhadamuth; and we are still far from my city."

"May we have no more rain till then," I say fervently. I am so weary of dampness; perhaps it is even worse than thirst.

There is a compound where caravans may set up their tents; our bodyguards work with stakes and canvas while Beizun and I seek out an inn, eager for hot food, and there, over hastily commanded bowls of stew, we ask about schools of martial arts in the town.

"And what do ye want with fighters?" demands the tavernkeeper. "The ruler of this town allows no fighters save his own guardsmen. No mercenaries are allowed within the walls, and if ye are fighters, I'd suggest you keep it to yourselves or you'll find yourselves in his dungeons."

"What tyrant is this?" Beizun asks. "Does that law apply also to harmless travelers?"

"It does. He fears that someone will send an army to topple him from his high seat, so he has made a law that no one may enter the city wearing any weapon bigger than an eating knife. Your swords, gentlewomen, must be left at the gates when you enter the city."

I say to Beizun in an undertone, "Let us stay outside the city, then. We can surely buy all the supplies we need in the bazaar outside the gates."

But Beizun is indignant.

"He has no right to make any such law," she insists. "We should teach him better manners."

Nevertheless, when we walk up to the gates a guard steps us and demands that we leave our weapons there in his custody.

"Over my dead body," Beizun says wrathfully. "I am a free woman of Rhadamuth, and no man may lay hand on my weapons."

"Then bear your weapons away to wherever you choose, outside these walls," says the guard, "but through these gates you do not come with sword in hand."

At last Beizun turns away, fuming. "The arrogance of that man," she says, "Never have I heard such a thing in any city where I have traveled!" But if there are no schools of fighting, we have no business in the city, and at last we turn aside into the bazaar where we seek a comfortable place to lodge; we have not slept under a roof since the ill-fated night at Dargan's inn, and we long for a comfortable bed in a room with dry sheets and a good fire.

And so after an hour of looking about the bazaar we find ourselves in the common room of an inn, with hot soup and a room commanded where we may sleep warm, and we hear the men in the inn discussing the ruler of the town, Kerrak by name, and his unwelcome new policy that none may bear weapons within his city.

I sit and listen with my feet to the fire, drowsily enjoying the warmth. Into the room comes a wandering peddler, with a tray of bracelets and cheap trinkets. Beizun calls him over, and looks through his tray of bracelets made with small colorful pebbles, far from jewels. "Look, these are the same color as your eyes, Zadi'," Beizun says, and I take up the earrings she pointed out, pale-gold lumps of resin.

The peddler says, "You have chosen the one thing of value on this tray; amber from the Northern forests," he says. "This jewel is from ancient resin of a tree; look, here within it is the shape of an ancient insect caught within the resin when is hardened."

It is like a blow; suddenly I know I have worn amber before this, and why.

"It is my name," I say, in a low voice which I can hear trembling. "Beizun, my true name is Amber."

"A beautiful thing for a beautiful woman," says Beizun, and buys the earrings for me, touching my earlobes gently. "See, your ears are pierced; before this, you must have worn earrings, my Zadi'," and he puts the earrings into my ears. The holes are old and half closed; the wires stick and she has to turn and twist to get them in; I whimper and protest, but at last she finds the direction of the pierced holes and they slide in easily.

Once in, they feel right, and I touch them wondering.

"Amber," I say in wonder, fingering the lumps of resin hanging from my earlobes. "I am Amber."

And with the sounding of the word a dreadful anxiety comes over me. I am Amber—always I had thought that if I could remember my name, the rest would come with it. But I am no nearer to knowing why I am here, or how I lost my name and background. I fall asleep still compulsively touching the smooth lumps in my ears, knowing I have worn earrings before this, formed of the jewel whose name I bear . . . but when and where is still a mystery to me, as much a mystery as ever.

We linger before the fire, enjoying the sensation of being dry and warm before going to a dry bed; after days and days of sleeping in a damp and moldy tent in blankets never completely dried, the thought of a warm and dry bed is luxury beyond dreams. Our own company is sufficient; two drovers come and offer us drinks but we refuse politely.

"Perhaps we had better go to our room," I suggest to Beizin after this. "Women alone in a drinking-place are always assumed to be in search of male company."

"Then they can damn well learn different," Beizun says sharply. "We've as good a right

here as any man, and the same right to choose
our own company!"

I know she is right, but I dread the confrontation. Again I sigh, knowing she has more courage than I will ever have. I do not really want a
drink, but I accept one anyhow and sip at it
while Beizun drinks, my fingers restlessly twid-
dling the lumps of amber in my ears.

A shadow falls across us: a tall figure in
mannish breeches and boots, but the delicate
long fingers and smooth texture of the skin tell
me this is no man. "Will you ladies honor me
by joining me for a drink?" she asks. "And may
I sit here with you?"

"It is a public room; the chairs are not mine,"
Beizun replies. "Sit wherever it suits you,
madam."

The stranger sits on the bench next me,
stretching out her long legs. "Did I not hear
you, earlier in the day, protesting the law forbidding weapons within the city?" she asks.

"You did, lady," Beizun says. "A foolish law
and all too evidently a law created by a fool;
who is to say what a weapon is? I know fighters who could kill with a shepherd's crook;
will that fool of a ruler therefore forbid every
old granny to carry her walking stick? I have
been schooled in the art of killing with the bare
hand; will he chop them off at the wrist? The
law allows an eating knife; but I have known
men who could sneak up on a sleeper and cut
his throat with a knife no longer than I would
use to trim my fingernails. A foolish law."

"You'll get no argument from me on that," the stranger says. "My name is Reri, and the tyrant who has pressed this fantastic law on the city is my brother Kerrak."

"Brother or no, the man is a fool," Beizun says, and Reri nods.

"He is worse than that; he is a usurper," she says. "My father had no legitimate sons and I am his lawful daughter; when my father died, Kerrak bribed some of the Council to say that no woman could lawfully succeed my father— although there have been many Queens of Arkavan in history, the last of which was my own grandmother. Bribed by Kerrak they had me exiled from my own city—I would have been killed, but escaped that fate because many of the elders of the city remembered my grandmother's rule and were not averse to a queen rather than a king. They told me I should think myself fortunate that I escaped death or imprisonment. And now I hear of this absurd law he has passed forbidding all weapons in the city. My brother is a coward as well as a fool."

"He fears then that anyone bearing a weapon might endanger his rule?"

"I can think of no other reason," says Reri. "He knows I am a better fighter than he, and if I should challenge him to single combat there would be no question about the outcome. Since we were children I have been able to trounce him thoroughly, barehanded or with any known weapon. And he knows it, and fears the loss of face should I do so publicly."

"A curious story," Beizun comments. "Yet I ask why you told it to us—or do you tell it to every stranger?"

"Not so; but I see by the weapons you bear that you women are warriors," Reri says, "and I felt perhaps you might have some feeling for a woman ousted from her legitimate place."

"Even if we sympathized with you entirely," Beizun answers, "what good would it do? Even if Zadieyek and I managed to smuggle our weapons into the city—and this is no quarrel of ours— how could two women alone recapture your city from Kerrak? Be reasonable, Lady Reri."

"First tell me, are you mercenary soldiers?"

This time I answer. "We are not; we are slaves of the Lady Ifania, who is kinswoman to the Akharet of Jemmok," I tell her. "And we are seeking other women gladiators to fight for her in the arena."

"You will find none here," Reri tells us, "for my brother has also banished all teachers of martial arts and arms-masters, saying his is a peaceful city."

"Peace is a good thing," says Beizun, "but in a country like this I can see that it might be folly; suppose his country is invaded after he has disarmed all his citizens?"

"If that happens he is lost anyway," says Reri, "for his people do not love him and will not fight for him."

"This still sounds hopeless," Beizun says. "I think you might do well to journey to another city and try your fortune there, Lady Reri."

"I will not leave my father's people in the hands of tyranny," Reri says stubbornly. I do not see that she has a choice, and I say so.

"You would need a powerful army of fighters," I say. "Have you any plans?"

"First I must find fighters for my cause," says Reri, "and when the city is in my hands, then I will deal with my brother."

On that note we bid Reri goodnight and go to our own room.

Early the next morning we find Reri in the common room before us, and while we breakfast on boiled eggs and fresh-cut melons from the bazaar, Beizun ventures, "You are seeking women for fighters, as also are we. Why should we not travel together?"

"Agreed," Rezi says. "For I had intended to go to Gyre and to Rhadamuth, where there are traditions of fighting women. You seek women to fight for glory in the arena; I, to fight for gold in the recapture of a city. I cannot see why any woman—or for that matter, any man—should choose the arena unless the alternative is death or worse; if fighting is your chosen avocation, why not do so for a better reward than you would find in the arena?"

"I agree with you, if one has a choice," Beizun says. "Zadieyek was given none. I thought the arena better than any other alternative offered to me."

"Perhaps if I were offered that choice, I should choose the same," says Reri amiably. "Believe me, my friends, I meant no slight to you or your choice."

"I am happy to hear it," Beizun says with a menacing gesture, "since we did not go into the city and are still in possession of our weapons."

It is agreed that we shall travel together at least as far as Rhadamuth, Beizun's home city, which lies at the far end of the great desert. Remembering the nightmare of captivity, thirst and rape, my heart sinks at the thought of crossing the desert, even in the company of these two brave women, one of whom is my friend and lover.

Reri is familiar with the desert; under her tutelage we make some purchases in the great bazaar; cloth water-bags of coarse canvas which will keep our stores of water cool by evaporation, special fodder for our beasts, a tent of a lightweight material to keep us cool in the hot desert nights. She is introduced to our two remaining bodyguards; they stare curiously at her, having never before, I suppose, met a woman, even a woman fighter, who affected the wearing of men's clothing. For herself Reri equips herself with sword and fighting-staff. There is no lack of good weapons outside the city.

At last all is ready, and we load our purchases, and ride along that rocky trail which leads to the great desert. Under the brick archway which shelters the entryway to the bazaar, we sit on our riding-beasts, looking at this barren land devoid of all vegetation or any mark of the habitation of mankind. Bare and hopeless as it seems to me, with a trail barely marked in the loose sand, winding away into the distance of a barren horizon, Beizun welcomes it; this is her home country and she sniffs at the hot and scentless air as if it held rare perfume, shakes the reins of her riding-beast, and takes her place at the head of our caravan, as we ride out.

The riding is hot and wearying, and although I have been warned to be sparing with the water, my mouth quickly becomes painfully dry. I put a coin in my mouth and suck on it to keep my lips moist; fear of thirst is worse than thirst itself. The glaring sun beats down on my covered head until my hair is damp and streaming with the sweat that runs down my neck. We pause at the sun's height to eat bread and dried fruit, and drink sparingly; the sun makes me feel too sick to eat, and Beizun tells me to eat salted dried meat. "You lose the salt in sweat, and that is what makes you feel ill," she scolds me. "But you must eat."

"Look," Reri says, pointing to the southward, "the sun is covered with clouds; perhaps it will be cooler."

Beizun looks to the south and turns whiter than I have ever seen her.

"Those are not clouds," she warns. "It is sand—the devil wind of the desert. When it reaches us nothing can live." She gestures to our bodyguards to unload the tent and set it up; "It may be our only hope." The men scoff at our fears, and in the end Beizun sets up the tent herself, dragging inside our supplies of food and water, and before we have finished the wind is already blowing, fierce cold gusts laden so heavily with sand that we find it hard to breathe.

"Inside the tent, quick," Beizun commands. "The beasts are born to this weather, but nothing human can survive." She all but grabs the bodyguards and hauls them both, protesting, inside.

Even inside the tent the air is already so laden with sand breathing is difficult. We soak our veils in water and hold them over nose and eyes, to keep out the grit-laden wind, but gusts of wind blow so loudly that we cannot hear one another speak; the wind shakes the tent like earthquake, and at the height of the storm, a fearful gust tears it loose from the moorings and down it comes in a smothering mass over us, burying us in its folds. I struggle to get loose, from the suffocating weight of canvas weighting me down. When at last I writhe free I thrust out my head into a maelstrom of sand that blows over me with such ferocity that I no longer wonder that it blew down the tent. I am surprised only that the tent did not fly away on the wings of the wind entirely.

Frantically I burrow beneath it again for safety as hours drag by—hours of raging wind and shattering fierce gusts of sand. It is the nightmare of my first days; somewhere in the dark nightmare, suffocating in terror, my throat raw with sand and thirst, hands touch me in the darkness and I scream with the old panic:

White fire splitting my head, hands fumbling at me—the endless nightmare of thirst and heat and violation. . . .

"Zadi! Quiet, it's all right—" In the smothering dark I recognize Beizun's voice and touch but it is moments before I can control the whimpering moans I hear from my own throat. When will I be free of this nightmare from the past? Somewhere in the corridors of time past I hear a voice calling a name I now know to be mine:

"Amber! *Am-ber!*" But there is no more than this to the memory, just the sound of a name in what I fancy to be love and longing. I try desperately to put a name or a face to the voice, but there is no more, just the voice of another lonely ghost in the haunted echo chamber which I have instead of a past, a voice calling my name.

Beizun holds my hand now in the dreadful darkness, trying vainly to quiet me, to comfort me. What a friend I have found in her! "What is it, Zadi? Why were you screaming?"

"The old—memories—" I stammer. "The desert—"

"It's all right, don't think about it. You're here with me and I won't let anyone touch you," she promises.

I gasp for breath in the folds of canvas enveloping us, fight my way to a breath of air.

The storm is over; the air no longer fills my lungs with grit. We squirm our way into the open, and look out on a scene of desolation; all signs of the trail are gone, we are alone in a great unmarked waste.

The men haul at the folds of the tent, manage to clear it away. Food and the precious waterskins appear undamaged; the beasts stand, rumps presented to the blistering wind, chewing their cuds, as if no wind born of the desert could ever ruffle them. We have survived the devil wind all but unscathed.

But the trail is gone; only the trackless sand and the stars above remain.

"Don't fret," says Beizun. "If we follow the rising sun, we are sure to come upon the trail."

"And it is past midnight, I know by the stars," says Reri. "The sun will rise in a few hours."

It is far too late for sleeping. The men pack up the tent, load the animals, make a fire, with little bricks of hardened charcoal, and we cook soup. Everything tastes of dust and there is grit between my teeth. The water with which I try to wash it away tastes of warm stake leather but at least it is wet. Reri and Beizun repeatedly swig from a wineskin, but when I try I hate its dry sourness and spit it out in distaste. The weight of my weapons wearies me. Beizun and I pack our swords and shields on one of the beasts. The men, finished loading, come and squat by our fire. Reri dips them out bowls of stew, hands them the half-full wineskin and tells them to finish it. I do not begrudge them that.

A dim red pallor to the edge of the sky shows where the sun will presently rise; Beizun points and says, "There lies the way to Rhadamuth!" Wearily we haul ourselves into our saddles, turn the unprotesting animals to the east, and begin the journey anew.

I am weary and my haunches ache with the long hours in the high wooden saddle. The smell of dry desert sand and vegetation drags my thoughts backward to that first journey. I am luckier than I would have believed; from the repeated rape, I might have become pregnant by one of those men whose very faces I have resolutely blocked from my mind. That would have prevented me from becoming a gladiator; nor would I, I suppose, have lasted very long as a harlot. I never believed that I would think myself lucky. Yet this morning, as the sun rises, I know I am fortunate to have a kind mistress who loves me, a friend like Beizun, and even, to a limited degree, freedom.

And now I have a name, too, from before the white fire dividing my life. *Amber.* I finger the glassy lumps of resin in my ears, and reflect on the name. Yet I suspect to Beizun I will always be Zadieyek, as I am in the arena.

It is a good name. Yet when I reach Gyre, will I perhaps find friends, family, a mother even, or a former owner—assuming I am a slave—anxious to contend with Ifania for me?

Knowing I am valuable is soothing to my mind; I sway drowsily in the saddle, and jerk myself awake just before I fall off. A sleepless night had done me no good. Reri, too, I can see, has mastered the knack of sleeping in her saddle, a matter of adapting herself to the motion of the animal beneath her, and after a time I master it too and fall into sleep, automatically readjusting my posture from moment to moment in a dark dream.

I rouse when the animal beneath me slows to a stop, and come awake, glassy-eyed with weariness, as the animal settles to its knees to let me get down. I slap at the beast as it turns for a contemptuous bite, and am nipped in the wrist for my pains. Reri insists on washing the wound with wine, which stings, and bandaging it with a strip of toweling. Thus hampered with an aching wrist and a bandage, I am set to stir the pots while supper cooks, while Reri and Beizun climb the summit of a nearby hill to scout out landmarks for the next day's journey. I rinse my eyes with a little of the precious cup of water given each of us; it is worth the thirst to see clearly without grit grinding the inside of my eyelids.

Beizun comes running down, triumphant. "Bless the man who laid out this road so straight," she cries. "We are no more than a thousand steps from the road where it runs clear to Rhadamuth!"

The men are off-loading the animals, stowing the loads inside the tent they set up. When we have swallowed the stew made of dried meat and coarse vegetables, and almost quenched our thirst with the single cup of water each, we lie down to rest, we three women in one tent and the men in the other. Just as I am dropping off to exhausted sleep I remember our weapons, that the loads have been shoved into the tent where our bodyguards sleep. It is the first time since I came to the House of Fate that I have slept with my weapons out of arm's reach, and it troubles me.

But I tell myself that since Beizun and Reri have dropped to sleep without worrying about it, (and they would know if it was not safe) I am being overly cautious, and at last I sleep.

I wake and for a moment I do not know where or who or when I am; I stir drowsily, and a heavy hand covers my mouth. I gag and kick, and feel the edge of the knife at my throat.

"Don't stir," growls a harsh voice. "We don't want to hurt you, you're much too pretty for that. We just want a little fun with you. —Halet, tie up the other redhead and the one who wears breeches like a man—this one we can have some fun with, she's too pretty for a fighter!"

I twist silently, trying to bite. Halet swears as Beizun wakes while being tied, and lands a fist in his face. Angry now because of his bleeding nose, he twists the cords dreadfully tight and I hear Beizun swearing in an undertone.

Now the hand of the one who holds me rips down my sleeping-shift, and roughly parts my thighs. I arch frantically, and manage to kick him where it will hurt the worst. He howls, clutching himself, and staggers back into the darkness; my wrist aching, I struggle to get to my feet, and when he comes at me again I find the skill in my arms and hands; without any conscious thought, I strike out and hear his neck snap with an audible crunching sound. The other man, kneeling over Beizun now, turns to come at me and I discover I have flung him across the tent with a gesture that sends pain lancing through my bitten hand. Moonlight lies across the floor of the tent; Reri is sitting up staring at me in dismay.

"You've killed them," she accuses.

"They meant murder, or at best rape," I remind her. "Could we take them, imprisoned, all the way to Rhadamuth?"

Beizun asks, "What will Ifania say?"

"When she knows what they tried to do," I say, "she will understand."

Together we drag the dead men out of the tent and lie down to sleep again. When I wake there is bright hot sunlight and we begin another day in the desert: we leave the bodies for the buzzards and other desert scavengers.

"Tonight," says Beizun, "we should sleep within the walls of Rhadamuth."

In fact it is just past noon when at the edge of the horizon we sight low walls that enclose the city of Beizun's birth.

She says to Reri, "There will here be no nonsense of being parted from our weapons," and it is true. The guards at the gates of the city, tall and formidable in their armor, are women, and for a moment, looking up at them, I am troubled; but then I remember how without thought I killed both of the guards. I could do the same with these, even armed as they are.

I have never before given any thought to my fighting skills; now I have discovered that within me there is obviously a fine-tuned killing machine. Why? And where did I acquire the skills that allowed me, that first day in the arena, to pick up a weapon and kill my assailant with it? Even worse, if I had that skill within me, why, during that first trip across the desert, did I allow myself to be repeatedly raped and driven, captive, through hunger and thirst and abuse? There is confusion in my mind. I finally decide, when I have battered my mind repeatedly with the question, that the white fire splitting my mind must have been some form of explosion in which I was injured and left in such confusion that I—or "Amber" as I seem once to have been—forgot the fighting skills till they surfaced under stress in the House of Fate. I wonder if *Amber* is a common name in Gyre where, I understnad, women are routinely instructed in self-defense and fighting skills.

But the armed woman soldiers of Rhadamuth fill me with a sense of—I don't quite know— *rightness*, such as I never felt in the arena. Always there was some unfelt indignation teasing at me in the House of Fate, which said, deep on a gut level, *people should not have to live like this.*

I feel no such inner revulsion against the women soldiers I meet, armed, at the gates of Rhadamuth. Instead I feel open admiration. One of them recognizes Beizun and rushes at her, enveloping her in a great hug. They prance around holding each other, and finally Beizun remembers us and introduces us as old friends. The woman soldier is named Kezia, and Beizun tells us that they have been friends all their lives. "Our mothers were pregnant at the same time and laid us together in one crib; we are all but sisters," she says. "Kezi', this is Zadieyek of Gyre, a fighter in the arena in Jemmok."

"Does the Akharet still keep to that loathsome custom of enslaving all strangers to fight in the arena?" Kezia asks.

"He does; I sold myself to the arena to keep out of the copper mines," Beizun tells her, and Kezia frowns.

"Gambling again? I told you one day it would ruin you." Kezia admonishes.

Beizun says, "Don't scold me, sister. I am free of the arena for the moment at least, for Zadi' and I were sold by the Akharet to Lady Ifania, a fan of the arena who has a passion for woman fighters; she sent us out of the city to recruit fighters for the arena. And this is Reri, who travels with us, and like us seeks women— not slaves, but mercenaries to recover her city." She tells a little of Reri's story, and while Kezia listens, summoning her fellow guards to listen too, I wonder if I also am of Rhadamuth, so comfortable do I feel with these women. I want to ask Kezia if anyone in her city has missed a daughter or sister by the name of Amber.

But when at last I gather up courage to put the question to her, Kezia looks at me kindly and says she has never heard of anyone bearing that name.

"So you have lost your memory, but retained memory of all your skills as a fighter? I have heard of such things; the body remembers when the mind does not," Kezia says, and embraces me.

"If Beizun is your friend, you are my friend too, and my house and all that I possess shall be as your own," she says. "And also, any fighting woman is my sister. And as for Reri, I cannot go and fight for your city, for I have given my pledged oath here; but perhaps we can find some fighters who are free to go and help you to recapture your birthright."

"I regret that greatly," says Reri, "for I would welcome you as the first of my army; but I respect your pledge. And I will welcome any friend of yours and guarantee good wages and plenty of fighting and plunder."

"And now," Kezia says, "coming from the desert you must be parched and weary. The tavern we used to frequent still sells the best beer this side of Gyre itself, and the innkeeper still welcomes us there." She arranges with one of her fellow soldiers to take over her duties—she is a kind of corporal or petty officer of the guard—and leads us toward the tavern.

Inside it is cool, and they bring us great pitchers of beer and also, when I refuse beer, of a drink made with lemons and filled with clinking ice; nothing within memory has ever tasted so good to me. After the desert thirst I drink till I feel that I will slosh if I walk.

It is agreed that we will, when we have rested a little, make the rounds of the schools of fighting in Rhadamuth. The sun has angled down a little from the midheaven, and we can walk in the lengthening shadows. I walk between Beizun and Kezia, feeling comforted and content.

In the first of the fighting schools, I see only women. The owner of the school laughs at me when I ask about men. She says, "I never take male students for every midwife and every mother knows that men die more easily than women while girls are hardier as children and stronger when they are grown." Nor does she think they can make satisfactory fighters.

This seems reasonable to me. In the rounds of the schools we find a woman willing to fight in the arena of Jemmok, though her mother and the head of the school are both appalled; she is lured by the thought of gold and jewels, the knowledge that—if they live—gladiators mostly buy themselves free, already rich, within three years. She is willing to risk three years of her life for riches; I think she is a fool.

"You did it," she says to me.

"I was given no choice, except the choice to be a gladiator's harlot, but you have a decent life here."

"Nevertheless," she says, "I would be neither

the first nor the last woman to risk death for riches and fame," and I know this is true. There is nothing I can say to dissuade her.

But we find no others, nor any willing to fight as mercenaries for Reri's kindgom, in making the rounds of the nine fighting schools within the city. I wonder if the men here feel as strange when they think of men fighting as I did of women when Beizun first came to the arena.

It is agreed that we shall spend the night in the barracks as Kezia's guest, and on the morrow begin the long journey to Gyre.

Inside the barracks, Kezia and Reri await us, and Reri is fuming because, she says, she has heard a fantastic story in a tavern.

"These people were trying to tell us that the world goes round the sun," she says, laughing scornfully. "When any fool whatever can see that the sun rises in the morning, and sets in the evening so it must therefore go around us."

And at once I know precisely what is meant.

"But the world does indeed go around the sun," I tell her. "I can prove it to you." And I pick up a piece of fruit from the sideboard, and stick a pin in it. "Look, here are we, and Beizun, take this lamp. . . . you are the sun" I say, and I walk slowly round her, pointing out. "See, it looks indeed as if the sun rose and set over the world, but it is the axial tilt of the planet which creates light and dark." I take a stick of charred wood from the fireplace and draw a crude diagram of sun and planetary orbits on the floor, remembering from somewhere a model where sun, planets and moons revolved round and round one another. I even remember the name they give such a device; it it called an orrery, but I remember nothing more; how is it that I can remember this complicated device when my own name and parentage are unknown?

Reri stares and says "There was once a philosopher at my brother's court who said something like this. Where did you learn this?"

I suddenly remember being a small child in a roomful of other children, watching as a teacher explained it, just as I had shown it to Beizun and Kezia, with a piece of fruit and a candle. I said "It was shown to me as a child, in a group of other children," and the old frustration, why cannot I remember where and how? Like the sound of the name *Amber*, it is hidden somewhere in that unknown past before the explosion of white fire devided my life into *now* and *before*.

In Gyre then will I find some clue to my unknown, unguessable past? Even to myself I do not propose the question of what will become of me if I do not.

It is decided that we shall set off for Gyre in two days; we must replace supplies and go into the markets of Rhadamuth to trade one of the riding beasts which is pregnant for a sturdier one. As we are engaged in this, a woman comes to us, shrouded in thick wrappings and veils.

She asks Beizun: "Good woman soldier, are you going into the desert?"

"A reasonable question with these animals," Beizun says, "but no, lady, we are bound for Gyre."

"How much gold would you ask," she continues, "to let me travel in your company?"

Beizun looks at me, questioning. I nod and she says, "I am desperate to reach the city of Gyre to rejoin my husband."

"It is not a matter of gold," Beizun says slowly. "But we travel in haste. Can you ride hard?"

"Oh, yes," she says quickly. "I can travel at any pace you ask."

Something in the way she averts her eyes as she speaks lets me know she is lying. I wonder if she is lying about her husband, or if she has never before been on the back of a riding-beast.

Well, whether or no, we are saddled now with the woman; she goes to collect her possessions— "One bag," Beizun warns her seriously, "we must not encumber ourselves with much luggage," and she agrees demurely, her face still hidden from us behind her bulky garments and veils.

When we speak of her to Reri, Reri fumes and suggests we leave at dawn the day before, to avoid her.

"Who is that dame anyhow, and why are we to take her with us?"

We know nothing but the name she has told us: Mikhala. An unfamiliar name, but she seems desperate.

"Beizun, the trouble with you is that you are too soft-hearted; always a soft touch for a pretty girl. Has she lovely eyes or something of the sort?"

"And if I am," Beizun says, "suppose that I had refused to have you in our company?"

"Why would you refuse me?" Reri asks, with the unconscious arrogance of a queen. But that is what she is, of course. . . .

They argue about it for half an hour or so, and I finally shout at them.

"What does it matter? We are not in so much hurry as all that, after all. Two or three days will not matter to us or to Lady Ifania, if we can there find fighters she wants. No matter how badly this woman rides, it will not make that much difference. Why not show the same kindness to her that we would wish for ourselves? She would not, after all, wish to travel with a caravan of men—or have you forgotten what fortune we had with those so-called bodyguards hired by Lady Ifania to protect us?"

"Zadieyek is right," Beizun says. "We will still have time to search for fighters for the House of Fate, and the mercenaries you wish to restore your kingdom. True philosophy is to render to others that which we would wish for ourselves."

"I would not have treated those bodyguards that way . . . in truth, what they had planned for us was what they would have wished, whereas what we wished was to be let alone," Reri reminds us, but I protest. "She is but a small woman, and fat too—I doubt she has any skill in fighting, and if she did, and should try to attack us, Zadieyek, who is the smallest of us, could wrap her up in one fist and not so much as be short of breath."

Thus admonished, Reri shrugs and says, "So long as she does not expect me to carry her baggage, then, or bring three dozen trunks to be guarded."

But when we assemble the next day at the city gates, Mikhala is there, with a plump well-fed riding-beast and one single bag of possessions which, when I hoist it for her to the back of her riding-animal, feels as if it contained only clothing. . . . more clothing in that bag than I would think one small woman could wear on such a trip, but who am I to judge? My own clothing consists only of a few fighting-tunics for wear in the arena, and Beizun has not much more. Under the heavy riding-mantle that conceals her, I see a glimmer as of fine silk and guess that beneath the heavy cloak she is as finely dressed as Lady Ifania herself. This seems to me strange for a journey into unknown country; I wish I had courage to wear, like Reri, a man's functional breeches and boots. The road, unlike that which leads into the desert, is well-built and surfaced, wide enough (and smooth enough) that a donkey team could drag a great four-wheeled cart along it, and indeed before the day is out we pass such a conveyance, rumbling slowly along with a sound like thunder, moving so slowly, and taking up so much of the roadway, that we are forced to jog along awkwardly behind it, until we reach a wide place in the road where we can pass and ride ahead.

"A ladylike contrivance," says Mikhala with a faint shudder. "Imagine being a lady and being forced to travel shut up in one of those, jolting the breath from one's body!"

I do not think it would suit me either, but I have no memory of having traveled in such a cart and cannot say. In any case we soon leave the cart behind, and within a few minutes it is out of sight. But something is nagging again at my memory; I may never have ridden in a donkey-cart but memory teases me with the memory of some windowless vehicle more confining than the cart. Bits and pieces of memory are surfacing from the mysterious time before the explosion and fire split my life in two. I am almost afraid to mention it to Beizun; but when we camp that night in our tents, I nestle close to her and whisper my fears; that I will not find my memory in Gyre, that I will not find it anywhere.

She soothes me with caresses, and I confide my worst dread; that I will discover that I am a slave to some man who would use me like a harlot.

"Is the thought of a man so dreadful to you, my Zadi?" she asks me gently, and because of the way I have been treated on that first trip through the desert, I can only cling to her, trembling, without even strength to confess the fear.

"But you must not be so frightened; men do not harm you and most of them would take no pleasure in the thought of an unwilling woman," she reassures me. "You have only had bad fortune in encountering evil men; most men, my dear, are good and harmless."

I find this hard to believe.

"If it is so," I challenge, "why then do you seek lovers among women?"

She laughs and confesses that she cannot answer. "But I have always been unlike other women," she says. "Most women would complain more of a man's indifference or neglect than of his attentions. And perhaps if you belong to some man, as slave or as wife, you will recover your desire for him as well."

To me the thought of desiring a man seems even more strange and frightening than being taken unwilling as I had been. I should be thus an utter stranger to myself; this has become so much a part of my life.

Since leaving Rhadamuth the desert is gone, and I observe the change in the character of the land with amazement. We travel through a land where hills rise, one after another, each a little higher than the last and sometimes at the very top of a hill we can see a view of distant mountains very far away. I wonder if these beautiful hills are in the land of Gyre and whether the faint haunting nostalgia and admiration means they are the hills of my homeland? For Reri and Beizun find the sight cold and depressing; they have no love for the distant skyline of high, toothed ridges of mountain.

The road alone remains, built heavily with blocks of stone, and once I ask who built it.

Those who came many, many years before us, Beizun tells me, an ancient Empire who conquered all the territory between Rhadamuth and Gyre; this sounds also vaguely familiar though I have no spontaneous memory of the name she tells me.

The riding animals fare well on this smooth surface and we make good time, but Beizun's fears about Mikhala are soon justified; she rides badly, lagging sometimes so far behind that we fear she will lose sight of us entirely. Still she is a cheerful companion, though I wonder how she can continue to shroud herself in the thick riding-mantles which all but conceal how small and fat a woman she is. To me the heat is still painfully confining, and I throw off all but my thinnest tunics—as does Beizun—for here are no men to see and perhaps be inflamed or tempted. I ride beside Mikhala now and then and encourage her to keep up, and under the thick hood which protects her from the sun, I see her face red and beaded with sweat starting forth; yet even when I urge her she will not remove the mantle.

She tells me little of herself, except that she is rejoining her husband in Gyre who is (so she tells me) a carpenter and builds furniture for the markets; he owns, she says, a little shop near the city wall. I wonder how he came to leave her alone in Rhadamuth and she tells me that her sister is a mercenary soldier in the city guard. She does not tell me, or Beizun, why she has chosen to travel at this season of damp heat. At night she sleeps alone in her own tent, though we have invited her to share ours, to save her the labor of putting it up; but she refuses more than once and at last I suppose that it may offend her that Beizun and I are lovers—though why a woman of Rhadamuth would feel that way I cannot imagine.

It is about the fourth night on the road when we come to a great river. We can see that once it has been bridged by the same people who built the roads, for the great stone piers remain and some fragments of the bridge-supports. Yet there is a great gap between the bridge arches here and the far end of the river. I wonder, facing this swollen river, why the bridge has not been kept up and maintained; but across the river is jungle, and Beizun tells me that this is the very border of Rhadamuth; that for many years the women of Rhadamuth guarded the bridge, but the folk of the jungle feared the fighters of Rhadamuth, and at last carried away the stone for building, hoping it would keep the people of Rhadamuth on their own side of the river.

"How, then, are we to cross the river?"

"There is a ford a little way down there," syas Beizun and points to where the stone of the road gives way to a deeply rutted and worn track leading away downstream. Following this new track we come at last to a shallow ford where the water just covers a set of stepping stones. I would think that the bridge should have been built here, but they assure me that the course of the riverbed had changed more than once since the people who built the stone roadway had their empire.

"Take care," Beizun warns us, "the ford is not as easy as it looks. There are deep potholes where if you lost your footing on a stone, you could drop in over your head; there are also patches of quicksand. It is safest to let the animals swim under us; they will try to pick their footing, but if they step off into deep waters they can swim, though they do not like to and will protest if we try to drive them directly into the water." She glances around to make sure no strangers are spying on the road and strips off her tunic. "My skin will dry faster than my clothing," she says, tucking the tunic into the small saddlebag of personal effects she carries before her. I follow suit and so, after a moment, does Reri. Only Mikhala remains shrouded in her concealing riding-mantle; it seems to me she must suffocate within it. Reri, at the head of the line, bashes her riding-beast on the head and he lumbers clumsily into the river, picking his way from stepping-stone to stepping-stone. A few stones over, he misses his footing, and goes down into a deep hole; off goes Reri over his head and into the water, and now I see the good sense of stripping to the skin, for she comes up snorting, flounders around, catches the bridle of her animal and chambers into the saddle unharmed. Warned by watching her, I am wary when I am pitched over my animal's hump, and submerge into the peat-tasting river; I struggle to the surface, discovering to my great surprise that I can swim, and grab at the saddle-prong. Beizun alone manages to cross without a ducking. Mikhala balances carefully on her saddle as the beast picks his way with clumsy feet along the stones, but her balance is bad—I do not think she can ever have been much of a rider. Off she goes, clumsily cumbered with her heavy robes, which all but drag her down under for good before I reach her and grab at the thick blankety folds of her clothing. I haul her up dripping and snuffling, the stuff of the riding-mantle dripping streams of water; I feel that I would like to pick her up and wring her out. The folly of such garments in the jungle heat has now been amply demonstrated, but she will not shed them even when I offer her one of my own tunics. At last we are all on the jungle side of the river, Rhadamuth left behind, and in the jungle heat Mikhala's robes do not dry, but steam; the air is so damp that there is no way for the water to evaporate. I slip my thin tunic over my head and again offer Mikhala dry garments, which again she refuses. I wonder if she is mad, or if she has some religious tabu against wearing any other garments than these; she seems to overdo modesty, in fear that one of us will catch a glimpse of her naked body, but even when we offer to put up her tent so she can change her clothing in privacy, she courteously refuses and begs us to take no notice. Later in the day I note that she is shivering; there are fevers in the jungle which she could have taken from her drenching, but she insists, when we stop for the night, that she is perfectly all right.

"I'm worried about her," Beizun says as we are putting up our tent. "Damn the woman, what can be the matter with her?"

"Stupidity," Reri says, "let her alone with her folly."

"But is she is ill, we will have, in common humanity, to lose time in nursing her," Beizun frets, "time we can ill afford to lose."

"Well, it was you who *would* bring her," Reri protests.

"It was only the humane thing to do," Beizun said, "How could I know she was such a fool?"

"In common humanity," Reri said, "I will brew an herb tea which will perhaps protect her from fever—if she is not too great a fool to drink it."

Reri is kinder than she sounds; she brews the tea and gives it to Mikhala, saying, "Drink it; it will protect you from the fever · you deserve after riding in wet steaming clothes all the day."

"Oh, you are too kind," Mikhala says gently. "You should not have troubled yourself."

"Damn right I shouldn't," says Reri, "but if you have fever we will have to nurse you, you silly girl. We can't afford to lose the time."

Obediently Mikhala drinks down the bitter tea, only grimacing a little as she hands back the cup.

Soon after she puts up her tent (again refusing help, though we can see how slowly she moves) and her face is again beaded with sweat. The sun is barely down. Beizun and Reri and I linger beside the campfire, watching as the stars break through the tangled boughs of the thickset trees above us. Then we put up our tents, Reri alone in hers, Beizun and I together. As we ready ourselves for sleep I can hear Mikhala moaning inside her tent and I call out to her.

"Mikhala, are you sick? Do you need anything?"

"No, I'm all right," she calls back in a strained voice. "Thank you. Good night."

"Sleep well," I call at last and she mutters something I do not hear clearly. I settle down, but the heat keeps me from sleeping, and again and again I hear Mikhala's moans which at last change to a harsh panting and gasping.

I turn over and try to sleep, but the maddening sounds continue. Then comes a hoarse wailing scream, and at my side Beizun sits straight upright.

"What in the name of all the devils—?"

"Mikhala," I say. And the cry comes again.

Beizun calls out to her: "Mikhala?"

At the same time Reri calls from the other tent, "What's wrong, Mikhala?"

After a moment her voice, strained and wavering, "Nothing. I'm all right, leave me alone."

"She sounds as if she were being visited by demons," Reri mutters, and when the hoarse scream comes again, there is no hesitation among us; the three of us together burst into her tent.

For the first time we see, by the light of the tiniest of lamps, Mikhala without her riding-mantle; and also the reason why she would never take it off in our sight.

Mikhala lies writhing on the floor, her breath coming in gasping moans. Her body is naked, with the huge distended belly. Beizun curses softly; none of us would have taken a woman this far into pregnancy on such a journey, for fear of just such an occurrence.

Reri kneels beside her and asks gently, "Is this come much before you looked for it?"

Mikhala gasps, "Only a few days; I was sure I could reach Gyre and—and my husband."

Beizun says grimly, "You should have stayed in Rhadamuth with your sister, if she is not just another figment of your imagination. Didn't you know that riding would bring on premature labor like this? And if it hadn't, a fall and drenching like you had today, would have done so. Little fool, to endanger your life and the life of your child like this!"

"Is there much danger?" Mikhala asks.

"Why ask me? I am no midwife," Beizun says crossly, "nor is Zadi'."

"Nor I," Reri says, "though I have seen births enough among my women. Tell me, Mikhala, is this your first child?"

"No, I have a daughter four years old, with my sister in Rhadamuth," Mikhala says. "And she was born easily, so I thought I could manage this time without tending—"

"'I fear this is just what you will have to do,'" Beizun says, but her tone is gentler than the words, and as Mikhala gasps with the renewed pains, she gives her her hand to hold.

I wish I could go away, where I need not hear or see the inexorable process taking place before our eyes. The night drags on; Mikhala gasps and cries out and moans and sometimes she screams, and an hour before dawn, she gives birth to a small, red, bloody child.

"A daughter," Reri says, lifting it up to inspect it, after which she cuts and ties the cord and lays it in Mikhala's arms.

"A daughter," Mikhala repeats. "A warrior woman for Rhadamuth, then." She bends over the small wrinkled red face as if it were rarely beautiful. Something inside, a gut feeling, tells me that to Mikhala the small wrinkled face is beautiful, ugly as it may seem to one who has never been a mother.

I take the babe reluctantly into my arms and wrap it in a clean fragment of nightgown, and stare into the small wizened features. How curious, that this little button-sized nose, these miniature feet which seem too tiny to consider that they can ever be walked on, may some day be a copy of Mikhala herself. Reri comes back with a cup of one of her herbal teas for Mikhala.

"Drink it, and go to sleep," she says. "We will not travel today. What do you think you would have done had you borne this babe in secret as you thought you could do? Were you intending to smother it at birth, or expose or abandon it?"

"Goddess guard us, no!" Mikhala says with all appearance of sincerity, clutching the swaddled bundle to her breast? "What kind of woman do you think me?"

"God knows," says Reri, "A woman of iron, if you thought you could travel on within an hour or so after childbirth."

"I can do what I must," Mikhala says angrily, "and you made it so clear you were in great haste—"

"I think you a fool," Reri says, "but I cannot fault your courage. It will not harm us to lose a day," she adds, "Drink this, and rest."

Mikhala sips at the tea, hands back the cup, and falls asleep with her child cradled against her breast. Silently we slip out of the tent, leaving her to sleep.

10 Three days later we see in the distance the great stone gates of Gyre. Mikhala is still shaky on her feet, but she had clung to her saddle gallantly for the last two days.

Since Hassim first told me that I fought like a woman warrior of Gyre I have longed for this moment, certain that I will know the gates when first I saw them. But the gray fog, the white-fire curtain across my life does not stir or shake when I behold those great rising pillars of rose-red stone. They are simply high walls and pillars and gates of wood ancient and blackened, fastened with hasps of bronze, greened with age. They are not at all as I pictured them. I am, on the contrary, all but certain that I have never seen them before.

Dark falls before we reach the city, and we

begin to camp outside Gyre, but Mikhala insists that we continue. She has still not told us why she did not remain with her sister until her child was safely born and old enough to travel. Now she tells us, her face clamping tight with rage.

"A friend," she says, scowling so that we know she means the very opposite, "made sure I knew that Kal had taken another woman into his household. And I would not let him excuse himself by letting it be thought I had deserted him."

And so we ride on as the moon rises and the stars come out, and pass through the gates of Gyre, riding through the dark streets at Mikhala's direction, until we draw up the animals at a small townhouse behind a metal-barred fence. As we dismount, two fierce-looking watch-dogs set up a loud barking and come rushing at us; then suddenly they stop, fall silent and begin frisking around Mikhala, licking her hands and trying to lick her face.

"There, good dogs," she whispers. "Bounce and Tiger, good fellows, it's all right." She carries the baby girl in her arms; beckons us to follow inside, through a large central atrium. From one of the rooms off the courtyard we hear voices and see light; Mikhala beckons and we follow.

Inside the lighted room there is a bed; Mikhala rushes toward the woman and man sitting up in bed with a platter of fruit in their laps.

The man raises his eyes at the intrusion and

stares, then stammers sheepishly "Mikhala, I
thought you were going to stay with your
sister. . . ."

"Yes, I can see that is what you thought,"
she says, standing over them. "And I can see
how you have accepted my cousin as your kinswoman in all ways. How kind of you, Lana, to
keep my bed warm for me; and it is lucky I did
not come four days ago, or I would have had
far more urgent need of the return of my bed
than I do now. Here—" she jerks away fruit
tray and covering, ripping down the coverlet to
expose the man's nakedness; he looks helplessly at me and Beizun and Reri, but Mikhala
thrusts the swaddled child into his arms; "Here,
Kal, take your daughter, get acquainted with
her, I will take care of our—guest." She jerks
the coverlet off the woman, who indeed looks
very much like Mikhala. "If I might trouble
you for the return of my bed, and of my
husband?"

The woman is wearing an embroidered night-
dress with handsome decorations of flowers.
Mikhala comes to give her a hand as she climbs
out of the bed; she lays her hand on the collar
of the night-dress, saying, "if I might have my
gown? On second thoughts, Lana, keep it—"
and takes her hand away. "I do not think I care
to be troubled with washing away the smell of
your perfume." She wrinkles up her nose. Then
she picks up the tray of fruit. "How kind of
you to make such a fresh sweet bedtime snack

ready for me." She takes up a mango and begins to peel it.

"Mikhala, have you no shame?" groans her husband.

"It seems to me I should ask that of you, Kal," she says, laughing, and clambers into bed beside him.

Just then the infant sets up a loud wail, and Mikhala turns and takes it from her husband, uncovering her breast to feed it. The wailing subsides and Mikhala demands, laughing, "Now get this woman out of my house before I set the dogs on her! They were glad enough to see me home, they will certainly drive away anybody I want driven away!"

Kal comes, grabbing up a random garment to drape his nakedness, and puts an arm round the woman. "Lana, I think perhaps you had better go—"

"Indeed she had," Mikhala says and laughs. "These three women with swords are my friends."

Lana looks at the three of us and visibly quakes, then turns and bolts out of the room. Outside we hear the dogs set up a great cry, and Mikhala says, "Kal, you had better go call the brutes off before they maul my poor cousin."

Beizun can no longer restrain her laughter; she guffaws and says to me, "Let's leave the lovebirds to their nesting, friends. Mikhala, if you ever want a place among my warriors, let me know; you have strength enough for any three women I know!"

Mikhala smiles and murmurs, "Why, Beizun, I am no fighter, but a simple home-keeping woman."

Reri giggles and says, "If such are the house-wives of Gyre, their warrior women must be frightful indeed."

We are still laughing so hard we can hardly stand up straight as we come out of Mikhala's house. Kal stands to call off the dogs, saying belatedly, "You are Mikhala's friends and you brought her across the wild country and cared for her when our child was born; can we not at least offer you lodging for the night?"

"I thank you," says Reri, "but I should think you would have had enough of showing kindness to strange women."

He looks so sheepish and shamed that I almost pity him. He cannot be all bad if Mikhala undertook the journey from Rhadamuth to keep her claim on him. But he looks foolish enough now.

Beizun says "Such help I would have offered to any woman in need of it, friend Kal; see that you offer no more insult to your good wife," and he bows his head and stammers. "Indeed it was not what Mikhala thought—"

"No indeed," says Reri. "I am sure you took the bitch into your bed as you would any puppy dog, just to keep her off the streets," and as we ride away laughing he stands embarrassed, head hanging and tail between his legs.

"So," Beizun says, "now we have had our adventure; our first move must be to find a respectable inn for the night, and tomorrow we begin our search for your past, my Amber, my Zadi'; someone in this town, I doubt it not, will be proud to claim you. There was once an inn run by the elder sister of one of my guard. If it is still there, it is clean and the beer's not bad. I think I can find it from here."

Despite the high moon, it is dark in the streets and twice Beizun had to stop and ask directions of a chance passerby. But finally we find the inn and command a room for the three of us and stable space for our beasts. There is only one bed for the three of us and against my will I am reminded of the night when Beizun and I both shared our mistress' bed. Nothing of that kind will happen tonight, I know; Reri has no sexual interest in women. As for me, though I admire her, I do not seek her as a lover. It is different with Beizun; we have been so close since first we met. I wish we were alone, and without meaning it, I feel resentment against Reri. When Reri is asleep Beizun draws me into her arms like a child and we sleep that way, entwined.

When morning comes we briefly argue about what we are to do first; Reri wants to seek mercenaries, while Beizun and I feel that we should go first to the schools of martial arts and sound them out about fighters for the arenas of Jemmok. In the end we take separate paths, agreeing to meet again that night at the inn for dinner, to share one another's success or failure.

We have been given directions to the largest school of martial arts in the city. Now it is so near I lose my confidence, I hold Beizun's hand as a child on her way to school clings to her mother.

She asks me, "When did you begin to fight?"

Without thinking I answer, "I got my first black belt when I was thirteen." She frowns and asks what is a black belt.

"A token of competence in fighting," I answer, but then I can remember no more. I fall into despair at the way snatches of memory come and go and nothing associates with them afterward. Yet it is there in my mind, clearly, the black belt tied around my waist, tied there by a man, and a row of other girls all older than I, in white fighting suits.

But I cannot see any single face clear, or remember any name but my own, and even that is hazy. Was my name truly "Amber" or is that a bizarre fantasy? My eyes blur in confusion and I can just make out the letters of the name of the school of martial arts, written above the door. We go inside. The mistress of the school comes to greet us, a tall broad woman with a face like a marble slab and she greets us courteously enough.

"How may I serve you, ladies? If you wish to take instruction in the arts of fighting, a class for beginners will open at the next full moon; I may have some places available in the advanced classes now, but I would have to examine you for placement and I have no leisure today nor tomorrow. If that is what you want, I will examine advanced pupils in three days, so you may come back then."

"Thank you," Beizun says, "but we have our own trainer."

"Then—?" The woman was still civil but a little impatient now.

"This request may seem strange to you, lady," I say, throwing myself into the confrontation, "but have you ever seen me before?"

She studies my face for several minutes and finally says, "I do not know. Your face is not altogether unfamiliar, but I cannot put a name to it. What is your name?"

"In Jemmok I am called Zadieyek," I tell her softly, "but I was in some sort of accident or explosion and my memory is gone. In my childhood, I think I was called Amber."

"You have the look of a fighter," she says, "but I think I would have remembered a name as unusual as Amber. No, my dear, I am sorry, I do not recognize you." She seems really to regret it. "Why do you think that you came from Gyre?"

"I was told in the House of Fate that my fighting style was like that of the women of Gyre."

"I am sorry, I wish I could help you," she said. "One of my students told me a few months ago that her sister had disappeared and that they had hired mercenaries to search for her. I do not think they sought as far afield as Jemmok, though. They described her as being of small and slender build, with red hair and brown eyes like yours. Perhaps you should seek her out at her house."

I ask her for many particulars until at last she says she must return to her students. She gives directions to the house of the student who had lost a sister, and I am lost again in the excitement of my daydream; I will walk into the house and immediately be recognized as sister, daughter, family member; in a few minutes I may well be in the arms of my mother. Though surely if I had had a sister I would have remembered?

The house is large and elaborate, more so than Mikhala's, and totally unfamiliar when we are summoned inside to wait for the lady of the house. My heart is beating so loud that I am afraid it will burst through my chest. In a few minutes perhaps I will be in my mother's arms. But when a quiet lady draped in gray comes into the room I signal despair to Beizun, for I have never seen her before.

In fumbling, half-stammered words, I explain our mission. She says kindly, "Poor girl," and strokes my hair. "My Lillia was older than you, and her hair not half so bright. "And you can remember nothing of your past? When did you come to the arena?"

"In the winter."

"In the winter, Lillia was safe at home with us," she tells me. "In early spring she ran away—or was taken—and we have sought everywhere. How my heart sprang with hope when I had the message. Poor child, I cannot tell you how much I too wished that you were my daughter come home." And again she strokes my hair. "You have suffered, I can tell. I hope you find your family."

I feel sick with disappointment. I would so willingly have accepted this kindly woman as my mother, this house as my home. But I am beginning to wonder if anyone will ever claim me, or if I shall spend my life in wandering and search.

A voice behind me cries out "Lillia!" and I turn, to see a young girl in a white tunic, about fifteen years old. As I turn her face takes on a look of great sadness.

"No," she says, "you are not my sister, though you are very much like her in build and coloring."

"I almost thought so too," says the lady, "and when I saw her, I hoped. No, we must accept it; Lillia is dead somewhere, and we will never know."

"And we cannot even mourn for her," says the girl sadly.

"Just the same, I would show you kindness as I would hope someone might do for Lillia if she were alone and seeking her family in a strange town," says the lady.

"Will you not make your home here with us
while you stay in Gyre?"

Beizun looks curiously at me; I nod, and
Beizun accepts, but tells her that this night we
must return to the inn to speak with our comrade in the search.

"And if anywhere in your travels, you hear
anything of my little Lillia, I pray you, tell her I
love her and await her return every day; will
you do that?" she asks, embracing me in farewell, and I promise.

We spend the rest of the day making rounds
of the martial-arts schools, and we find four
women eager to fight in the arena of Jemmok;
but nowhere did I hear of any other family
missing a daughter named Amber; nor did I
hear of anyone who had ever borne that name.
When we return to the tavern, Reri has re-
cruited seven mercenaries to follow her to her
kingdom, and asks each of our prospective gladiators if they will join her in her effort. Only
one accepts.

"If you had reached me first, I would rather
travel with you and help you recover your kingdom," she tells Reri, and turns to us. "Why do
we not go there first and when we have restored her throne, there will be plenty of time
for the arena," Reri says, and Beizun joins in,
agreeing eagerly. I am not so sure that this is
suitable; how do we know how long it will
take to recapture the city, and will Lady Ifania
be angry if we risk our lives except in her
service? But I am overruled; with the fighters

for the arena and the mercenaries, Reri says she has the core of an army, and we agree that next morning we will all go together for supplies for the siege.

I am not happy at the thought of leaving Gyre so quickly, but I have searched as much as I can; I could not, after all, go from house to house, asking at each dwelling place if the household had lost a sister or a daughter.

Beizun was wildly excited; she was looking forward to war. For myself I had no desire for a fight; I would have preferred to confine my fighting to the arena. But I can find no way to tell Beizun this. She seems to feel that I will find the same pleasure in battle that she does. Late the next night we are ready to go, and I go and take a tender farewell of Lillia's mother, who insists on giving me a short sword which had belonged to her daughter, and recommends me to every God and Goddess I have ever heard of, and a good many I haven't.

I am brooding again, sick with my disappointment, when we ride out of the city. Nowhere to go, not even an idea where to search next. Amber is not a common name in Gyre either, but in the dialect of the people I found a strange familiarity—I don't know why; like a language I had known a long time ago and was now relearning.

Back we tramp, across the jungle, our beasts slogging along with their hooves squelching in the muck. Back across the ford; through the hellish heat of the rainforest; at last we draw up outside the gates in good order, where Reri shouts a challenge of defiance.

"To that usurper my brother Kerrak deliver the message that in three days he shall meet me on this ground to do single combat for our city and the winner shall rule. And if he does not come out and fight, I shall come into the city and take it."

A clear tenor voice rang out from the heights above us:

"Reri, my sister, you are as great a bully as when we were both in the nursery! I do not admit that being more able than I to raise soldiers or to defeat me in combat will make you a better ruler than I."

"I am fittest to rule," Reri called. "I have led the armies of this city three times in battle!"

"And I have kept it in peace for three years," he retorted. "Let the people choose whether they wish a leader of war or a leader of peace!"

"What have the people to do with it and why should they choose? There are always more cowards than honorable soldiers, and what have they to say when the law has always been that the oldest child assumes command of the city? You kept me unlawfully from that place, brother."

And then there was a great outcry from the multitudes inside the city, and we could no longer hear the voices of individuals, not even of her brother.

"Who ever heard of letting the people choose their own leaders?" Reri mutters. "The law is the law, and must be obeyed; it was ordained by the gods that the oldest *child*, not the oldest son, shall be leader of the people."

It seems rational enough to me that the people should choose whether they want a peaceful man, or a warrior woman, to lead them; but both Beizun and Reri seem to think of this as a fantastic idea.

At last there is a shout that encourages us, and we look up to see a young man standing on the wall; there are cries of *"Kerrak!"* and *"Reri!"* and then in the silence, Kerrak—for it is he—calls, "Will you come into the city and parley, my sister?"

"On the contrary; will you come out and fight, my brother? For if I should come into your city, only the gods know when or how I should leave it."

"And if I come out there to fight you, I know perferctly well that I should never re-enter my city alive," says Kerrak. "Why should I fight you?"

"To prove to the people of the city that you are no coward," shouts Reri.

"Oh, but I am a coward," Kerrak admits quietly. "I see no reason to be otherwise when we are not at war."

"Shame to you, then," shouts Reri. "Consider yourself at war, for I will never set aside my lawful claim to the city."

After a little time Kerrak shouts back, "I will not fight you. I willingly concede that you can

beat me at single combat; you have been doing
so since I was eight years old. But so be it, if
you want the city you will have to come and
take it."

And he jumps down from the wall to land
inside the city out of sight.

Reri stands looking at the wall where her
brother has disappeared. "And that is trying to
fill my father's place and rule the city!" she
murmurs. "Even the people do not fear him as
they should. He has curried favor with the people and is willing to let the rabble choose! I am
shamed that he is of our blood!" Abruptly she
raises her head. "Well, my warriors, will you
follow me? We need not fight, because he has
banned all weapons inside the city; so if we
seize a few strategic points, we will have no
trouble except to seize my brother himself."

She kneels on the ground and picks up a
long stick.

"Here is the north gate; we are at the south.
You seven—" she indicates the warriors from
Rhadamuth— "go round and take it. Zadi', here
is the palace; you and Beizun come with me.
Here are the granaries and here the main Temple." She looks at the women from the fighting-
schools of Gyre. "That will be for you. Hold
that place till I send for you when the city is in
our hands. Do you understand?"

She approaches the gate, and I feel the tight-
ness in my stomach that I felt during my first
fight in the arena. This is no game; this is real,
and even though the people of Reri's city are

unarmed, I know they will oppose us. I do not think much of the policy which keeps the citizens unarmed; they cannot ban every butcher's knife, every pitchfork, every shepherd's sling or staff.

Reri throws up a rope with a hook over the wall, and goes up it hand over hand. Two welcomes await her; as her head crosses the wall to where it is visible inside, a shout goes up "Lady Reri! We will fight for you!" and almost at the same time I see a great rock or paving-stone come flying at her head; she ducks it easily, but if it had hit her it would have knocked her down into the city street. Beizun says, "Come on," as Reri beckons from the top of the wall, "Listen to them shouting; she's got some support inside there anyhow!"

Beizun climbs hand over hand and I swarm up the rope after her, cautiously not raising my head till I can see the crowd gathered below. They seem mostly women, a few men gathered but without weapons; a couple of them try to block Reri's advance physically, shoving and pushing, but she draws her sword and spanks them out of the way with the flat of it. Scorn, rather than fighting fury, is on her face as she leads the way up the long avenue toward the palace. She beckons to me and Beizun and we stride at either side up the street. Once a man leaps into the road and attacks us with a staff; Beizun quickly drives him off.

As we set foot on the flight of steps leading to the palace, Kerrak is there before us. He is a slightly built young man, richly dressed, with a jeweled circlet around his elaborately curled hair, which is redder than Reri's and his face more delicately pretty. She takes him firmly by the shoulders and sets him out of her way.

"Kerrak, don't interfere. The city is mine, but I have no wish to hurt or kill you." She listens for a moment for cries from the crowds in the streets, then says, "The north gate is in the hands of my women, and the temple, and the granaries; will you surrender with grace?"

He grits his teeth and says, "What good would it do for me to fight you?"

"None whatever," Reri says, not unkindly. "I have been able to defeat you at arms, as you said, since you were eight years old and I was ten. And I think you will concede that since I blacked your eye when you were thirteen or so, I have never hurt you. Now, as you see, the city is in my hands without a drop of bloodshed, which should prove to you that I bear your precious subjects no ill will." (We found later that this was not entirely true; a few men who held the north gate fought hard enough that one of the mercenaries from Gyre had had to wound one man rather serously and he afterward lost the leg from blood poisoning; but no lives were lost.)

"And," said Reri, "an army of men might have plundered and ravished the women of the city; but we have no intention of that. We mean you and the people no harm; but you must yield the throne to me."

"If I must, then I must," said Kerrak with a look of dismay. "but it troubles me, Reri, that you will lead my people back into the old warlike ways."

"Damned right I will," says Reri. "Suppose it had been an army of desert nomads at your gates, rather than I with my women? Would you have surrendered to them with so much grace?"

"How do I know what I would have done? It has not happened," says Kerrak, "I still do not believe that fighting is the answer. Nothing was ever settled by violence."

"You are mad, brother. Everything has been settled by violence since history began."

"No, my sister," says Kerrak gently, "You are wrong. For a settlement by violence provokes only another outburst of violence to overturn it. And nothing is settled for good until it is settled right."

There seems great logic to his argument, though I am not sure what good his logic would have done against an army of desert bandits who would not listen to it.

Kerrak leads us into the palace and an array of women comes out, shouting with dread, subsiding when they discover that the invading army are all women. They are Kerrak's queens and official consorts, and a small army of young children. At Kerrak's word they come forth one by one and promise to obey Reri, as the new ruler. They look confused and I am not surprised; if the city had been conquered by men, they would have been property of the new ruler.

Now they do not know what is to become of them or of Kerrak.

"What am I to do with you, then?" Reri asks. "I would gladly make amnesty with you, my brother. I bear you no malice now that you have yielded up my rightful place, but if you took oath to be my subject I do not think I would believe you; I know that if you forced such an oath from me I would not consider it binding."

"I will take no such oath," says Kerrak, and again I am favorably impressed by his straight-forward honesty.

"At the very least," says Reri, "you must accept exile for a year or more. Suppose I proclaim that if you are seen here within the city within a year's time you may be killed by any man's hand?"

"I would not fear that," says Kerrak, "No man in the city would lay a hand on me, and you know it."

"True," Reri says, troubled, and glances around. Beizun can no longer be silent.

"Lady, if we who took your city for you were men, you would certainly have given us our choice of the women—"

"I had forgotten, Beizun," says Reri, embarrassed. "Shall I then give you choice of my brother's women?"

"Not so," Beizun says. "They are interested only in men and they would not want me."

Then she says to me, "But what about Kerrak? Zadi', shall we take him home as a present for Ifania?"

"Just so," I say, delighted at the thought. "Her nurse Hatara has been nagging her for years to have children, and this one is at least of a royal line and beautiful—"

Kerrak protests, "But I have a wife already—"

Beizun says scornfully, "You do not think the Lady Ifania would want you for a *husband*, do you? When she is tired of you, she can send you back to your sister. But I think she would rather enjoy the loan of him as compensation for the use of her gladiators."

Reri shrugs. "Take him, then, to the Lady Ifania with my compliments and thanks."

Everyone seems content with this except Kerrak, who still looks troubled. Now the crowds around the palace begin to break up. One woman comes and clings to Kerrak, at which he seems a little embarrassed, and finally kisses her and bids her a very decisive farewell. She moves away reluctantly, and we are summoned to dine in the palace with Reri and her mercenaries.

We ask them at dinner if they wish to come to Jemmok for the arena, but they refuse one by one. We have the four women from Gyre who are already pledged; they do not comprise a *tammarim*, but they will be enough to fight under Ifania's colors in the next Games, and perhaps she will find others.

The banquet drags far into the night, Reri and her mercenaries exchanging stories of far-off battles and fights, and Beizun joins in, giving story for story, and even as the banquet extends into the early hours of the morning, challenging one another to fights in fun; a game which Reri stops quickly, since all of them are drunk, and sends us off to a luxurious room in the palace, where Beizun falls asleep quickly, snoring.

When she is asleep I see movement in the shadows and call angrily, "Show yourself! Who is it and what are you doing here?"

By the light of the single candle still burning I see Kerrak.

"My new mistress did not tell me what do do or where to go," he says. "I have come to her for orders."

"Well, she's asleep, and I don't have any for you," I tell him. "Find yourself somewhere to sleep and come back in the morning."

And as he goes away I reflect that everyone now has what she wants, Reri has recovered her city, Ifania is on her way to having her *tammarim*, but I am no closer to finding out where I came from or who I am. Except for my mistress, no one cares whether I am alive or dead, or would know. Yet somewhere I must have had a family, friends ... am I to wander all over the face of this world seeking them, or resign myself to being abandoned, orphaned?

Come, come, I admonish myself, it is not as bad as that. Perhaps my family died in the explosion of white fire dividing my life in half; and I am no worse off than others who have been orphaned in some calamity and have had to build new lives for themselves. I have my dear mistress and I have Beizun and Hassim, and there are surely many who have less than this. I creep close to Beizun and sleep.

11 Morning sun wakes me; Beizun is still sleeping at my side, but as she wakes she draws me down for a kiss, then looks past me.

"What is he doing here?"

"Kerrak? He came last night to ask for orders."

"I didn't send for him because I thought he might like to spend a last night with his wife."

As we watch him, Kerrak sits up sleepily from where he has found a place on the floor in a stack of cushions. Beizun beckons to him, and he comes to join us; Beizun holds out her arms and he crawls into the bed between us. With a kindly possessiveness she strokes his strong bare shoulders, and I watch, a little dismayed, as he begins to caress her. I do not begrudge her fun, but I would rather not be present.

He touches me, perhaps even by accident, and when I flinch asks gently and apologetically if he has hurt me.

"No, no, really you have not," I reassure him, and Beizun tells him in a whisper something which makes him lean over and give me a long gentle kiss. I am angry at the excitement I feel in spite of my wish to remain aloof. Somewhere deep in the remotest part of myself I feel that for me this is wrong; but Beizun coaxes me to join them and at last I am held between them, each of them caressing me.

"Please . . ." Kerrak begs, and while I murmur, "No, please, no, Beizun, don't let him—"

"Zadi', love, it's time, really. He won't hurt you and you can't go through life being afraid of one of the best things the gods ever made—"

Playfully, but with real strength he holds me down, and the thing is done, the thing I have feared since I wakened to it from the white fire in the desert; Beizun bends over me, kissing away the tears I cannot hold back. She is so far right, he has not hurt me, there is not the pain or panic of those other times, only the dreary sense that what I have done, playfully and to please her, is for me *wrong*, unendurably wrong, a crime for which I cannot even imagine atonement. I cannot give way to it, rejoice in it, take pleasure simply as Beizun does. Nor do I have any sense that for her it is wrong, I would have been glad to share *her* pleasure, make love to her alongside him, hold her in my arms while she loved—only that for me, it is forever a forbidden thing. Later when we are dressing I try to tell her this, but for the first time she has no understanding, no sympathy, only congratulating me for finally overcoming whatever it was that held me back. .

And without understanding why I am simultaneously ashamed and a little proud of myself that I have faced the terror and overcome it. Then I think of Hassim to whom I denied this, and who accepted my fear and my refusal; Hassim, the first friend of this, the new life over which I have so little control.

Perhaps now I can give to Hassim what he desired of me. But I am still in deep conflict about the wrongness of it, and I wonder why. As I finish tying my braids, I reflect that this is something every other woman seems to take for granted; is the answer hidden somewhere in the mists of my other life? And if I have forgotten why it is wrong for me why is it possible for me to be tormented, even obsessed, with the mind's unwillingness to follow what gives the body pleasure. For I do not deceive myself, there had been pleasure where I feared pain, and it is the pleasure I now fear, since I had survived and learned to endure the pain of rape. Now I am a stranger to myself, and why in the name of the gods they call on can I not understand why I have this sense of having trespassed unforgivably?

The mirror shows me the same invulnerable Zadieyek I know, but something within me has changed, I have lost something I can never reclaim.

Yet to everyone else I am the same, as Beizun and I gather our women together for the return to Jemmok—and the arena.

I am still troubled about the desert crossing, the heat, the prospect of another sandstorm. I wonder if Ifania will be angry that we have lost the bodyguards she hired for us. All day we are loading the riding animals, gathering supplies of water, fruit, food for the beasts; but now there are six of us with the women who have agreed to come and hire themselves—not as slaves but as free women—to the arena in Jemmok. Reri summons us to her new throne room to bid us farewell; she takes affectionate leave of her brother, embraces Beizun and me, shows us the courtyard before her palace, where her woman mercenaries are instructing reluctant citizens in the preliminary arts of defense and offense.

"And never again will travelers be expected to check in their weapons at the city gates," she says, gloating. "Come back to us soon, Beizun. I have good use for you."

Kerrak is all but in tears. "I created a city of peace, and you are creating one of war," he mourns. "May it be on your head, Reri, my sister, and may you get enough war to make you repent your policies."

"Your evil wish is more welcome to me than any good wishes I could have from such a fool," she says disdainfully, but she gives him a loving embrace and presents him with sweets and rich clothing for the journey. Her gifts to Beizun are jeweled weapons and an antique and fantastic set of armor made apparently from the scales of a prehistoric fish.

As we are mounting for the journey, overlooking the court where Reri's women are instructing the citizens in arms-play, which she has made compulsory, Kerrak joins us, richly garbed, and people line the streets, crying out "alas, our beloved and peaceful prince is leaving us!"

I care nothing for their prince. Now I am aware that again, for the third time, I am to cross this wretched desert of thirst and sand and hateful memory. I do not really remember that first crossing, only fragments of horror and pain, thirst and violation.

Yet this time it is different, I ride between Beizun and Kerrak, and in the night I sleep in their arms. The fierce desert wind dries my throat and my tears. And in dreams white fire explodes in my head and I search down dream-corridors for something I have lost; waking, I know it is myself I seek.

Days across the desert, and I see the towers of Jemmok, and the spire which crowns the House of Fate, where first I found myself and became Zadieyek, the person I am now. And in the deep aloneness of that night, waking while the others sleep, I step outside into the star-sprinkled and unfamiliar night above me, and know that the search is meaningless. It does not matter who I have been; Amber is the past, Zadieyek, warrior, is who I am now, and who I will be in the future is now in my own hands. I may be slave, and yet I have never been so free as now. Standing under the stars, I clench my fists and spit silent defiance at the white fire which shrouds my memory.

Far away on the edge of the desert I see a light hovering above the towers hidden in the darkness. I watch the slow-moving light, and find a strange question in my mind.

I did not know that this planet had satellites. Why have I never noticed them before?

And then the puzzled question; why, suddenly, do I know what those lights signify? Surely I must have seen them whenever I looked out at the stars. Surely this must be some fragment of memory from *before*, like the name *Amber*. Somewhere in the depths, memory must be stirring, and another curious concept comes into my mind; *lacunary amnesia, expecially when induced by trauma, is invariably temporary.* I do not know what the words means, but they comfort me. So I return to wondering if Hassim, sleeping in the House of Fate, has forgotten me.

And then silently I steal into the tent again and curl myself inside my blanket and sleep, remembering that when morning comes I will be again in the only home I have ever known.

We enter Jemmok in mid-morning, the high scorching sun blinding us as we pass beneath the Akharet's banners. In procession, trailed by children and curious onlookers, vendors, beggars, we tramp through the streets to the house of Ifania. She hears the commotion in the street outside and runs out to meet us. Someone in the crown has recognized me from the arena and shouts. "Zadieyek! Dreadful woman! You have returned to our city!"

Ifania advances to meet us; she looks at the strange women, gestures to me and to Beizun to descend. We dismount and salute her, bending low as the custom is, and Beizun says, "Behold, mistress, four women for your tammarim."

Ifania replies so softly that only the three of us can hear, "The best news is that you are safe."

Aris runs from the house and flings her arms around me. I see that she has grown taller now, taller and stronger. "Zadi', I am to fight for the first time in the arena in the games three days from now," she tells me, and I am overcome with dismay; remembering the tall young man who died in his first fight, I am overcome with fear for her. She is so young, not even full grown.

I wonder if she has the faintest idea what it means—to be a gladiator, to fight in the arena. Does she see only glory, or is she aware of death's face over her shoulder? I feel dread and the smell of death is suddenly in my nostrils, looking at her slender girlish arms and legs, the gentle swell of her breasts.

As the caravan gently untangles itself, the

beasts collected by their owners, our goods unloaded, Beizun moves a little apart to speak privately with our mistress.

"We have brought you a present, Lady," she says, and beckons Kerrak forward. He kneels submissively, and Beizun tells Ifania who he is and how Reri came to send him as a gift, and for a moment Ifania's forehead draws together in a little frown and her nostrils flare, and I wonder if we have been too presumptuous. Then she sees the funny side of it, and laughs merrily.

"And what am I to do with this beautiful young man?" she asks Beizun.

"Lady," says Beizun, "since Nurse scolded you, and since she is already shopping in the bazaar for a bigger bed, we brought you someone to share it that she might approve."

Ifania draws Beizun into a hug and draws Kerrak into their circle. "You are generous, beautiful one," she says, and smiles at Kerrak, with an impulsive kiss. Then she turns to me. "And you, my Zadi'—have you missed me?"

"Indeed I have, dear mistress," I tell her, returning her embrace.

Now it is time that Ifania shall look over the fighters we have brought her, one by one. She calls old Marfa to examine them for strength and health, and has Marfa bring them down to the hall where Marfa sets Beizun and me to testing the new fighters with sword and shield. After a time she gestures to us to draw apart.

"None of them, I think, will be your equal in

the arena, Zadi'," she says. "Yet this is a respectable beginning for a tammarim, and with
training you may make a respectable showing
in the arena against the tammarim of the
Akharet's consort."

This is how I hear that there are to be games
within three days at the House of Fate, and that
the Akharet has brought many exotic fighters
from far lands; men who fight with ax and
mace, men who fight with nets and slings, arch-
ers even—how we are to fight against these I
know not since they can cut us down from a
safe distance. And in three days from this day
the Akharet's consort is to hold a great feast
where we are to go and demonstrate what we
can do so that the society folk may decide on
whom to make their wagers. I am relieved that
at least there is to be no butchery of helpless
dumb brutes in the arena.

And so it is back to the routine of training
again; enforced by old Marfa, a sparse diet of
baked fish without spices, of little bread and
no meat, of vegetables boiled or baked, and a
little fruit; of cold baths to toughen muscles,
and massage, and worst for Beizun, of no wine
or beer; for me this is no hardship, and she
derides me when I drink water cheerfully; like
a dog, she says. The teasing is good-natured,
but I know it is a real hardship to her to drink
only water with her dinner.

Next morning in the courtyard we gather,
Beizun and I, with young Aris. She is eager to
show me her weapons; brings them to me as a

schoolgirl her playthings. Yet when she takes them up I see no longer the childish girl but the young warrior, in the first glow of her adult strength, and when Marfa puts us to practice together, I am hard put to it to maintain my ground against her; I have spent this last moon in traveling peacefully and I must suddenly gather together all the unpracticed skill; with a single swift rush Aris all but disarms me and I fall back gracelessly, losing my balance, so that when I recover I knock the weapon from her hand and then am overcome with fear that I have hurt her or killed her; she goes down and lies motionless, and I am suddenly overcome with dread; have my hands and arms so lost their skill that I must now kill or be killed?

I am suddenly filled with anger because she has made me display weakness and a return of fear. Are three days enough to recover my old skill? Could I bring myself, if it was the only way to save my life, to kill this young girl? And why am I now worrying about this? Surely my skill is great enough to preserve my life without killing, since it is an exhibition fight and not to the death!

But what neurotic desire to see blood shed has prompted the Akharet's consort to these imitation games? Perhaps Beizun, with her passion for gambling, can explain it to me.

I realize that I feel more resentment against the consort of the Akharet for her exhibition games, her imitation games, than against the Akharet himself for the true games in deadly earnest, life and death. And I cannot imagine why.

I wish that I could see Hassim. Perhaps I have dwelt too long in Ifania's house, this house of women. Perhaps fighting is a matter for men, and those who deride women warriors are right after all?

Marfa comes and pulls me round to face her.

"What ails you, Zadieyek, moping here like a broody hen?" she demands. "Come and work with Beizun; I want the newcomers to see the fighting style of Gyre."

Now I identify what it is that troubles me. "But I am not of Gyre," I tell her, "I found in Gyre no trace of my past, nor anyone to claim me as part of their life and family. I can no longer call myself Zadieyek of Gyre."

"And who is to stop you?" Marfa demands, "Can anyone give you a better name, or one to which you have more right?"

"That is part of what troubles me; I have no right to any name anywhere," I say.

She answers forthrightly, "Why should that trouble you? You are what you are, the greatest fighting woman of this season or any season from the House of Fate. Certainly you have the right to call yourself Zadieyek, Dreadful Woman, for there is no one with better right to that name; or whatever else you choose. What is a name anyhow? What difference does it make?"

I find it impossible to explain to her why it should matter to me that when I look into the mirror I should know who is there. Perhaps to her it would not matter that she did not know her name; perhaps it is only those who lack an identity who can understand what it is to have one or not. Once again my only value to myself or anyone is what skill I have as a fighter, and now again I must fight for the very right to draw breath. Perhaps if I had chosen to live as a fighter—

Then I remember that I did choose this life, such as it is, I preferred it to the other alternatives offered to me. And Zadieyek the fighter, little as it now seems to me, is the only identity I have, and at least better than none. And I must work hard, with these women around me, to keep that.

So I gather up my weapons, and prepare myself to exhibit my skill with sword and shield with Beizun. And as we stand toe against toe, facing one another, swords ringing on shield, something of the old magic returns, the pleasure in my own skill, the excitement of proving my strength and skill at every stroke. Neither of us can give an inch, neither of us can wound the other, or break through the other's invincible guard. Later we are separated, each pitted against one of the women from Gyre, and indeed I find that their fighting styles and skills are so like my own that it is very like fighting my own image in a mirror. Yet I have the extra strength and skill to know that none of them, matched against me, could break through my guard, and by the time Marfa calls a halt to the practice and bids us go and bathe and ready ourselves for dinner, I see them all looking at me with respect, at least, and some of them with downright fear.

Beizun and I are standing close together as, having been bathed, we dress ourselves in our finest tunics. And now I can identify at least some of my anger; that morning, with Kerrak, she persuaded me, against my will, into his arms. I must confront her about this, it is not right that anything should come between us this way.

I put round my neck the little crescent which was my patron's first gift to me, enjoying the glitter of its sparkle, wondering about the source of the crescent symbol; what does it mean here? As I stand on the balcony overlooking the courtyard, I look to where the moon is rising, and feel a sudden jerking sense of disorientation. Surely this is not the moon I have always known? The moon, the mysterious lights, somewhere back in my memory these must have some meaning. But when and where?

As I enter the dining room, Kerrak comes up behind me, winds his arm around me, kisses my neck with a careless assumption of intimacy which grates against my sense of rightness; I fling him off angrily.

"Keep your hands to yourself, or you will be picking them up one finger at a time," I warn him, and he looks at me like a whipped dog.

"What ails you? You were not angry at my touch this morning," he says, and reaches for me again; only when I back away with my hand on my dagger does he realize that I mean it and back away in confusion.

"I meant you no harm or offense, Zadi'," he says. "Will you tell me what has happened and why suddenly my touch offends you?"

Then I realize it is not his fault, and I smile at him, hesitantly. "No, it is not your fault," I say. "Beizun persuaded me; but remember, my brother—" for like myself he is, though born a prince, only a slave, and that bond of brotherhood at least we share—"this gave you no rights of ownership; touch me not except when I give you leave. If you can remember this, we shall remain good friends."

He casts a puzzled look at me, then at the hand on the dagger, and goes wordlessly to his place at table. Ifania has assigned him a place near herself, and beckons me to sit still nearer to her.

She looks me over with pleasure. "How that color becomes you," she says. "No less than Beizun; the two of you will do me honor in the field." And she touches the earrings in my ears, the lumps of amber which gave me the clue to my name, and says, "These are lovely, but I have not seen them before; how did you come by them?"

"Beizun gave them to me," I reply, and she leans forward, touching her lips to the pierced earlobes.

"Then she did well, for you are worthy of even finer adornments than these, my Zadi'," she says. "But I beg you, if you wish for jewels, ask me for them. It will be my pleasure to adorn you with the most beautiful things I can find."

So I know that she is jealous and "still infatuated" with me. I hesitate for a moment, wondering if I should tell her my true name and how I came to recognize it from the amber; but the moment has passed, for she has beckoned to Beizun to approach her; and is giving her some kind compliment on how well the green-blue silks suit her copper hair and fair skin. She has some kind words for every one of her new fighters, and when we have finished our dinner she calls us all before her and promises that we are all to appear at the consorts' feast a few days away, and promises that those of us who make a good showing shall have jewels and prizes.

"All of you who serve me well will find me a good and indulgent mistress," she says. "Though do not deceive yourselves, I will tolerate no rebelliousness or insolence; if any of you do less than you are capable of doing, you will wish you had chosen to end your days in the brothels of the lead mines."

Then she gestures forward a guest at the table who had not been introduced.

"The servant of the Akharet's consort," she says, "He has the schedule for the games, and you are to know against whom you are to fight."

Beizun has drawn the first lot; she listens patiently while it is read to her. She is to fight sword-and-shield against a sling-fighter, and I remember the young novice who was cut down in his first fight, underestimating the danger of the sling and the deadly little stones. I will have to tell her what I know and I wonder how this fight can be staged as a practice event and not a fight to the death. Cogitating this I hardly hear the sound of my own name; I too am entered for the games to fight sword-and-shield and I hear the name of my opponent as if in a dream: Hassim of Lerfaugh.

But this is not a deadly contest in the House of Fate; this is a demonstration fight for the pleasure of the Consort of the Akharet. I do not have to make a decision to kill him or be killed. Hassim, my first friend in this life, my dear comrade who taught me all the arts I know of fighting—except for those with which, it seems, I was born—or at least born into this life. Where I acquired them I still do not know and am now realizing I may never know. Although I am a fighter in the manner of Gyre, I did not learn to fight in Gyre.

An early bedtime is a part of our training schedules; Ifania, as the others are sent away, gestures to me and to Beizun and we follow to her chamber. I am not displeased with this, but when I discover that Kerrak too is to join us, I am troubled and I resolve that no matter what Beizun or my mistress may say, I will not allow him to make love to me this night.

This slips from my mind in the awareness of what my mistress Ifania is saying to him.

"You are handsome and nobly born," she

says, "and I have no children. Should you, Kerrak, give me a child, I will rear it in my house and assure that, male or female, it shall inherit all my property."

"My lady is gracious," he says in his husky voice. I see his eyes dwelling on Beizun, however, and suspect that his true interest lies there, not in my lady nor, thank all the Gods, in me. I hope, however, that this will create no dissension between my beloved mistress and my dearest friend.

I had believed that the nurse was joking about a bigger bed, but the one where Ifania awaits us is large enough, truly, to hold all of us with room to spare. She draws me close to her, and as she caresses me, she whispers to me, "I am a little troubled, for I have loved only women and have never been with a man before. Kerrak is handsome and seems a very nice young man, but I am still not sure—I would like very much to have a daughter or even a son of my own, but I know so little about men—"

I can understand her feelings, and I am eager to reassure her. "There is nothing to be frightened about," I tell her. Yet, remembering that first time in the desert, when I was terrified and fighting, I hardly know what to say to her. Because I know it is wrong for me, what can I say to Ifania, who has made this choice because of her desire for a child . . . ? I say, "Beizun can reassure you better than I. She has known the love of men and it does not frighten her."

Ifania holds out her arms to Beizun and

quickly it becomes a playful romp, as it has been before this with Beizun and me and Kerrak, multiple caresses, kisses, embraces, hardly aware of whose arms, lips, bodies touched, or how. I feel real tenderness toward both women, my friend and my mistress, and when Ifania draws back from Kerrak at the last moment, frightened, it is I who whisper encouragement to her; after all, I remember, this is intended for pleasure and did me no harm; and what she wants of him she cannot have without this. That she is still a little troubled I can tell by the way she trembles beneath him and clings to me; I want to reassure her, even to comfort her, but what can I say when this is something I have not chosen? Afterward when he turns to me I flinch and twist away from his kiss.

"But you told me all was well," whispered Ifania reproachfully, "and now you refuse what you encouraged me to share—"

I can only say, helplessly, that for me it is different, but I do not know precisely what I mean by it.

"You know I have lost my memory," I tell her. "I can only say that I have a real conviction that for me, somehow, it is forbidden, somehow wrong. I say nothing as to what any other may feel is right, but somehow for me I have a firm feeling that it is wrong. I beg you, my beloved mistress, do not ask me to do this."

"All the gods forbid that I or anyone should ask you to violate your own conscience," says Ifania. "One day perhaps you will know why this is so. Until then I will ask nothing of you, except your affection."

Beizun sits up, staring at me resentfully. She says, "Zadieyek, are you angry with me, then?"

"I was very angry," I tell her, "but done is done. I forgive you as I have forgiven my brother Kerrak. Only, I beg you, do not ask me again to give myself to any man's touch."

"I promise," she says. "I truly did not understand how you felt, and I would not for worlds have hurt you. I wished only to share one of the greatest pleasures I know, as I would have shared with you a fine wine you had never tasted."

Beizun draws me into her arms, and so we sleep, affectionately entwined together.

12 Dawn the day of the Games. When we gather together, the women from Gyre are troubled; they have never before fought in the arena, but only in the training school.

It is I who come to reassure them.

"This is only an exhibition fight; if you make a poor showing, if you are clumsy, the penalty is only that you make a poor showing, not death."

"But if we fight poorly, will Lady Ifania be displeased with us?" one asks. Already they all adore her.

Our training has been hard and continuous; we are all at top competence. The previous night Marfa had drilled us until long after the light failed, then dismissed us with a recommendation that we sleep alone, and I think if it had been within her power she would command rather than recommend.

With daybreak the house is all astir. All of us, Beizun and I, Aris and the four women from Gyre, are bathed, massaged, dressed like dolls in our fighting tunics, new and in Ifania's chosen arena color. Marfa comes to arrange our hair, and insists on clipping the hair of the women from Gyre almost to the scalp.

"For," she insists, "a foe may grab you by one of your braids and have you at his mercy. But Aris refuses.

"My hair is myself," she insists. "I will fight with it and if need be, die with it." And when Marfa comes at Beizun with her great clipper, Beizun roars at her:

"Take it away or I shall ram it down your throat. You will not touch my hair, nor Zadi's. You can intimidate those other wretches from Gyre, but I will go into the arena as a woman, not as a worker bee!"

"Well, there's no reason to shout at me," says Marfa primly. "I mean you well; I truly think it safer, and the mistress would be angry if I risked your life without necessity!"

Beizun says gruffly, "That's all right," and gives Marfa a well-meaning thump on the back that makes her howl. Then she comes and offers to braid my hair, as she has done before, more than once, and I am touched by the gesture. I remember the room by the pool, at the end of my first desert crossing, and the kind woman who braided my hair; and the day

Beizun first performed this sisterly office for me, my first real woman friend here. Memory stirring, I remember my first friend anywhere on this world, Hassim, and his kindness, and I wonder if I will see him at the Games.

When we are all dressed, Marfa checks belts, sandals ("Wait till the day a sandal-strap breaks in the arena—but when it happens you will probably not live to remember it") and makes sure all is secure and tidy; she removes jewelry from one or two of the women, scowls at the lumps of amber in my ears. "Take 'em out."

"Why?" I ask, and she grabs them and gives them a hard tug, which makes me yell in protest.

"Give your enemy no handles to grab you," she says, looking resentfully at Beizun's hair braided close to her head, and points to the scarred half-torn-off earlobe on her own head.

"A memento of one of my own fights," she says. "One I'd as soon have gone without."

Reluctantly I unfasten the glassy gems. They seem a key to name and identity, but when she pockets them I feel it is fitting. They belong to Amber, not to Zadieyek, who, no matter whence she may have come, is certainly not of Gyre.

And for today I am Zadieyek, all Zadieyek; no memories of that hidden other life which, the memory stirring, may soon reclaim me.

When all is secure and tidy, we are given our weapons. Mine, with the pointed shield, which has been polished and rubbed and treated with some substance which makes it glitter as if it had been sequined, I practically sparkle as I move. I do not know how it was done, but it is most effective and it will certainly startle any foe when I come against him.

The lights blind me as I step into the great open space where the games are to be held. I wish for a moment that it were the House of Fate which is known to me, where I fought twice and conquered.

In this smaller private arena there is no formal parade, but I see men drawn up at the far end of the arena in the purple of the Akharet, and in the crimson of his consort, or is it the other way round?

My imagination had failed at the idea of how they intended to present a sling-fighter as an exhibition fight, the sling-stones, hurled with such force, are inescapably dangerous. Now I discover the sling-fighter is armed not with stones, but with balloons laden with liquid dye, which give them a weight not dissimilar from his pebbles; the dye packets will shatter as they hit, staining everything with the dye, so the rules of the contest show that if Beizun's head is splashed with the dye, she is counted dead and the contest lost. Clever. I help to arm Beizun in her armor, and whisper to her that this is really a test of how well she can keep covered with her shield, until the slinger has expended all his allotment of stones—or dye-markers.

Beizun goes out against the slinger, who is the same little yellowish man I saw fight and kill within four whirls of his little sling, on the day of my first appearance in the arena. The crowd sees him and goes wild—he is a popular favorite. Beizun is greeted with equal howls, but I know that in her case it is a sadistic awareness that this is fighting for her life, even though the contest is not to the death, and I realize with dread that what they really want is to see a woman beaten and humiliated. Perhaps that is a universal desire—at least for men—to reassure themselves that any woman who dares to step out against them shall be so beaten, so humiliated.

In considereably less time than it takes to tell, Beizun has raised her shield, acknowledging the cries of the crowd as if they had all been encouraging her, and turned to face the slinger. He whirls his arm—too fast to see, it comes flying, but even faster, Beizun's shield is in place and there is a great splash of brilliant yellow dye staining her shield.

The crowd chants "One!"

Slowly, she circles, the shield held warily before her.

A second and then a third feint with the sling before he actually releases a second dye-shell to splatter on her shield.

The crowd chants ritually "Two!"

To me this contest is boring, with little at stake, and I turn away from the slow circlings, keeping track only by the shouting of the crowd. Some of them, I think, must be on her side now. At the chanting shout of thirteen—*fourteen is a tammarim*—I turn back as Beizun starts

advancing on the little slinger, the sword in
her hand raised and ready. The dye-splatters
are mostly on her shield—I cannot count them,
but I suppose the crowd has done so accu-
rately. Another whirl of his sling and some of
the crowd cry out;

"*Fourteen! A tammarim!*"

Beizun is ready to cast down her shield; she
is almost in top of the slinger when I realize I
have seen no splatter of fresh dye. A feint, a
trap! I want to scream to Beizun, but as she
begins to cast down her shield and run toward
the little slinger, I see the telltale movement of
his shoulders, and even before I can scream a
warning—but would she hear me over the
crowd?—the sling comes whirling and the final
pellet of dye splatters full across her face, over
the top of the partly lowered shield. The slinger
smirks; by the rules of the game she is dead. I
see the outraged, furious look as she wipes
away the dye, which has splashed in her eyes,
and is an irritant, almost a caustic. She plunges
toward the drinking pail, hastily splashing her
eyes, and I see her lips moving in curses; I am
too far away to hear, but at this moment I
would not like to be that slinger. He is already
strutting his victory, to shouts and applause,
when Beizun comes up out of the drinking
bucket and starts for him. She catches him
from behind, jerks him literally off his feet and
bending him across her knee, gives him a
half-dozen good hard swats with the flat of her
sword. The crowd, always ready for a joke—

expecially a cruel one—even on a popular favorite, goes wild and shouts her name over and over.

Yet there is an element of disbelief, even of disappointment even in this reversal, this just punishment, for the slinger's trickery; they wanted to see her destroyed, and since it was a fake fight and she could not be killed, they wanted to see her beaten and humiliated. They are furious at her recovery and revenge, even though it was justified. If the fight had been a real one in the House of Fate, Beizun would now be lying with her head split asunder. I remind myself that this episode will teach her caution for the next time she is pitted against a slinger, and may later save her life. She walks to the victor's spot—a few—including our dear mistress—are applauding fervently, and Beizun makes her a deep bow.

Now it is my turn. I walk into the arena and find that some are applauding us loudly. Hassim is grim and unrecognizable behind the face-protectors of his helmet.

It has come, the day I feared; when my dearest friend and I would confront one another, sword to sword. I lift mine in salute; he returns the salute and abruptly without warning, rushes at me. Even before I realize what I am doing, with no conscious thought, I catch his sword against mine, and the swords slide together, a deadly scissors approaching my throat. I push hard and get loose, turning warily, and as he spins we rush together and engage again. His strokes mirror mine; we are evenly matched, without, I think, the slightest advantage either way.

Though it is still early, the sun has entered the arena and I circle so the rising light will not dazzle my eyes. Hassim fights for the advantage, but I beat him back.

And I remember a frightened young woman screaming in nightmare, and Hassim comforting me, letting me curl, untouched, against his body, Hassim teaching me arms. Yet the superb killing machine my body has become keeps on fighting and I know it will continue, no matter what I want to do, to the very limits of my stamina.

I am weary, my arms tired from lifting the big sword, the shield everyone said was too heavy for me; Hassim's sword clatters against the shield and I am tempted simply to let it drop. What have I to lose? This is not the arena where a false move would mean death, I have nothing to gain by forcing Hassim to a technical defeat, nothing to lose by dropping my sword and letting him have such glory as he might gain from defeating Zadieyek.

Yet something inside me, like that inner resistance to allowing Kerrak the use of my body, will not let me lower my sword and concede the fight, though every muscle aches with weariness. I am not even certain what would be considered victory, what defeat; in the arena it would mean killing him, but here I suppose it will mean I must have him down and defeated to where any further move would mean *actually* killing him.

I make a savage swipe at his legs, and he jumps to avoid the sword; trips and goes down. Swiftly I take advantage, my sword at his throat, rolling him over on his back with my foot. Then I murmur so the crowd will not hear:

"Say the word and I will drop my sword and let you up and the fight can begin again."

But already the referee is at our side; he gestures to me to raise my sword so that Hassim can scramble to his feet, then he leads me to the center where I am acclaimed.

"Zadieyek! Zadieyek! *Zadieyek of Gyre! Warrior! Victor!*"

My dear mistress comes to lead me from the arena, to fling her arms around me, to hang a necklace of amber about my throat.

"It will match your earrings," she says, "And whenever you put it on or take if off you shall think of me." So I know she is still jealous of Beizun and wish I could reassure her.

"My warriors are covering me with glory," she says. "First Beizun and then you. I wish I could think of a suitable gift for Beizun; I love her too and do not want to neglect her. What, do you think, would please her best?"

"I think you should ask her yourself, lady; I do not think she would be shy about telling you," I say.

Ifania embraces me again. She says, "I can barely bear to send you into the arena again, for fear I should lose you."

I remind her that these are only exhibition fights and there is no danger of that. She hardly seems to hear me.

"You are scheduled for another fight, this afternoon," she says, and even for an exhibition fight I somehow have a fear that if you go into the arena, I shall lose you forever. I do not know why I feel that way, but I do."

I too am struck with an inexplicable premontion; that if I go into the arena this afternoon, something will happen; that Zadieyek of Gyre, who is not really from Gyre at all, will never come again to the life she has built here.

Nevertheless it is my fate; of my free will I chose to be a warrior and nothing else means anything in the face of that.

Then there are two fights between the men belonging to the Akharet and his consort, and the fighters of Ifania are allowed to go to the far end and sit down, to drink from the water-bucket (Marfa is there to keep any one of us with fights ahead from drinking enough to really satisfy our thirst) and to stretch out to rest. They are all full of compliments for Beizun and for me.

I close my eyes against the glaring sun, and wonder what is coming next. Sling-fighter against sword; sword against sword, sword against the exotic weapons I have just glimpsed in the arena.

I am no longer afraid; I have found my place, I am doing what I was intended by Fate to do.

As I lie here resting, letting my breathing slowly return to normal, I see a warrior in the purple garb of the Akharet's consort slowly crossing the sand.

The Games have stopped for an intermission, and in the stands above us patrician ladies and gentlemen are eating lunches, exchanging bets and gossiping. We are only toys to them; cherished and pampered toys, and again there is that strong basic awareness, we are human; *people should not have to live like this!*

The purple-clad one approaches hesistantly where I am stretched out among Ifania's women. As I had half guessed, it is Hassim. Marfa glares, but I gesture him to approach us.

"He is a friend, my dearest friend here," I say, and rise, to be seized in a warm embrace.

"I thought you would be angry with me," I say, "that I beat you in front of all those people."

"Angry? No, my Zadi', you beat me fairly," he says. "I hope the gods will be kind enough to grant that we never meet again on the sand, for on that day it would be my most unpleasant duty to kill you."

"Gods forbid," I say, and let myself remain in his embrace, held tightly, knowing that what is between us is, in many ways, perhaps in all ways, better than what I have given Kerrak and it no longer disturbs me that I denied, and will continue to deny this to Hassim. It does not matter; even between men and women, friendship is better than sex.

After a minute we draw apart and he laughs gently.

"But that is not what I came here for, my Zadi'. I have found out who is to be your next opponent and I came to tell you. I feared that you would worry about it."

Hassim is my friend indeed. I touch his hand lovingly and say, "That was good of you; only I hope you did not risk anything."

"Oh, no; only you know as well as anyone else that the lots are rigged," he says. "There would be no entertainment if two with no skill should fight each other, and there would be nothing much to see. The law requires only that no one who has his own fighters in the field should know beforehand, and perhaps spoil the betting odds."

I should have expected that. Those who romanticize sport should realize that all the clear skill is only in the service of corrupt men trying to enrich themselves; we gladiators fight and die, not for skill, or glory, but for the fall of a bet.

"And this fight is not even to the death," Hassim says. "They should not dishonor you this way, Zadi'; they have paired you with a novice to the arena, a lad who hardly knows how to pick up his sword. There would be small honor to you in fighting him, even if you were meeting to death in the House of Fate."

I have ceased thinking of honor. Nothing hands on these fights except the thrills for a corrupt hierarchy addicted to gambling. Nevertheless I will fight cleanly and honestly while I live, for my mistress and my own glory. And should I die, well, everyone must die some day, in some manner or other, and the death of a fighter at least is quick, without crippling diability or age or disease.

A bell sounds and I know this is the signal for the contests to be resumed. First there is a fight with quarter-staves between two who must be jugglers, for they fight with great slaps and whacks, taking fall after fall and wheeling away with comical gestures and somersaults; the crowd laughs and applauds mightily.

Then Aris goes out for her first fight, her short sword and shield borne as lightly as a schoolgirl's knapsack, her long braid bobbing. She has been pitted against a big warrior with an axe; they stand toe to toe and he whirls his axe with a blow which, it seems, must slice her in two; she jumps aside and catches the blow on her shield. I watch every move, holding my breath; I do not want the girl killed by accident, as she must surely be if she makes one false slip against the dreadful edge on that axe; it does not seem to me a suitable weapon for exhibition games.

Later, when he makes a fearful strike at her and her defense fails, I discover that for the duration of the exhibition games his axe-head has been replaced with one of wood trated with the same shiny stuff that makes my sword glitter. He strikes her and she falls; that is when I discover it is a wooden block, for there is no blood nor is her skull split apart; the referee walks over to her and declares the match a loss, and she returns to us, rubbing her aching head and crying in frustration.

Marfa says gruffly—she loves the girl, too—"You were lucky; another time your head won't be aching, it'll be lying where it'll never get back on your shoulders. Thank the gods for your headache, girl, and drink some of this, and try to rest and stay out of the sun."

And then it is my turn again. I study the young man walking toward me, and think perhaps I must also have a touch of the sun, for I seem to recognize his walk, to know him. He wears only the white tunic of the novice to the arena, and otherwise he is naked; a young man, hair dark and curly like mine, and he holds his sword, as Hassim had said, as if he did not know which end to hold it by. We come together and raise our swords in salute. Our eyes meet.

"Amber!" he cries out, "I wondered if it might be you!"

At once I know and recognize him and cry out his name.

"Jade!"

Weapons forgotten or fallen aside, we rush into each other's arms. I am home again, this is my friend, my sword-mate, my partner. He whispers, "We've got to give these people a show, Amber, it's what they came here for," and with a gesture I almost expect before he make it, I go flying over his shoulder, measuring my length in the sand. But I find myself rolling easily over, coming up to my feet as if on springs, rushing at him with the automatic cry;

"Hai!" and down he goes.

We have been matched like this before, I know; fought like this many hundreds of times. More than once, in fun—but in deadly earnest too—I have wagered my sworn virginity on my ability to defeat him; yet I knew myself in no danger, coming away from every fight virgin as I entered it, with no forfeit. For women of my caste, I remember now, were sworn while they still pursued the warrior's life, to remain untouched by any man. Thus my refusal of Hassim, my guilt over Kerrak.

Again and again we fling one another down, a practiced group of figures for exhibition fighting that keeps the crowd applauding and laughing, till we stand staring at one another gasping and smiling, neither willing to raise the hand that would concede the match. We stand leaning against each other, as we have done a hundred times in the training school.

I whisper "Jade, my brother, what are you doing here?" My voice is harsh with exhaustion, my breath barely sufficient to the whisper.

"Looking for you. Emerald and Beryl are across the river," he whispers, and embraces me surreptitiously. "And you? We were really terrified about you. What happened? Did the shuttle crash? We never heard anything—"

Now I know what the white fire must have

been, and the explosion which shattered my memory. Desert bandits who would not have dared come near a shuttle ship manned with the offworld weapons found it no trouble to rush the crashed shuttle on fire, pulling out booty beyond price, and the only surviving passenger. And she made it easy for them . . . memory gone, regressed to the state of a child by her head wounds.

I should have known they would have come to look for me—certainly the members of our sworn Group, three men and three women, masters of all the martial arts, intended—now I know it—to enter the arenas of this world and study what they meant. Even with my memory gone, I have fulfilled my mission.

The referee walks toward us.

"If neither of you will concede defeat," he says dryly, "I suppose I will have to call it a draw. Although this style of fight is unfamiliar, I cannot see that either of you has the slightest advantage.

We bow to one another in the prescribed formal manner and walk off the field arms entwined.

Hassim moves toward us.

"Who is this man, Zadi'?" he demands.

"My sworn brother-in-arms," I say. "More than blood-brother under our laws."

Jade smiles at Hassim. "A friend of Amber's is a friend of mine," he says, bowing.

And then Marfa comes up to me, to demand crossly, "What sort of exhibition do you call *that?* I thought you a warrior, not some kind of acrobat!"

I can tell by her cross tone that it is the worst insult she knows; yet I remind her, laughing, that she herself taught me acrobatics as a crowd-pleasing measure. Jade calls her gravely "Grandmother—" This in our society is a term of the highest honor though it isn't here; Marfa seems to know how he means it, and returns his amiable bow. "Believe me," he continues, "this is a fighting technique for killing with the bare hands, and more dangerous than a sword. If you wish, have anyone come at me with a sword and I will face him bare-handed and conquer."

Marfa says crossly that if she were the arranger of the games she would see him make good on that arrogant boast or pay with his life; but Jade has always had a gift for charming old ladies. Now I remember him using this talent on my own grandmother when he came to coax me to join our group on this mission; our family has never been among those who travel in space, for profit or glory, and I am their only daughter. It was bad enough that I had joined a collective martial-arms guild, and to go offworld was a family disgrace! Nevertheless in the end Grandmother had been won over by Jade's charm and even my mother had blessed my leaving, confessing that she truly liked my sword-sisters Beryl and Emerald, and giving the men, Jade, Ivory, and Agate, parting gifts as elaborate as she gave me.

Marfa leaves us with a scowl as Ifania walks across the arena. They are calling out the next fight, one of the Akharet's men against Beizun, and Ifania pauses to give her an encouraging pat on the shoulder as Beizun turns her steps toward the fighting arena.

I am still eager to know how Jade came into the arena, and ask him; he only whispers, "Long story," and turns to face Ifania.

"My lady mistress," I tell her before she can ask, "This man is my brother-at-arms Jade, and he has come to seek me."

Jade bows and adds, "I have sought her a long time; but when I came here to the arena, she had gone. So you are the patron who purchased unknowing a free woman, my sister Amber."

"Your sister? You are the son of her mother and father?"

"Not quite; but we are sworn as sister and brother," says Jade. He knows there is no way to explain to an outsider the concept of the sword-group; but it was because of our skill that we volunteered to come here and study the arenas of this worlds, an anomaly which still clings to this primitive society.

"You must allow me to ransom my sister, Lady," Jade says. "Whatever her price, name her and it is yours. If it is beyond the means I have with me, give me time to seek my family elsewhere—" we have no intention of divulging that we are from an alien sun, when a call on a carefully concealed radio would bring a shuttle down for us—"and you shall be fully paid."

Ifania says, with her customary petulance, "I don't wish to part with her. She is very dear to me—not a slave but a beloved friend. Will you family not allow her to remain within my household, if I formally make her free at once? Zadi', my treasure, do you really want to leave me?" she asks, holding out her arms, and I embrace her in return.

"It is not that I wish to leave you; but now I know this is not my home," I tell her truthfully. "I beg you, lady, let me go." And I kneel and place my two hands over my forehead as I have seen other slaves do but have not done myself till this moment. Ifania bends and lays her hands on my shoulders, remaining that way for some silent moments. At last she says, "If freedom and your family is your desire, my Zadi', then all gods forbid I should hold you against your will. But somehow I thought that your family had cruelly abused you and you had run away from them; for that reason I was glad to give you the protection of my house. And I cherished you as well."

"I know that, my dear lady," I say, and I know my voice is really breaking, "Be certain I shall never forget you."

"And the price?" Jade prompts.

Ifania waves her hands. "Since she was not legitimately bought from someone with the right to sell her, we will not speak of price. I beg you, let her freedom be my gift. And as for the

contemptible persons who ravished her and
sold her—you did not know? Perhaps the
Akharet could tell us who stole her from safety
and unlawfully sold her, with her wits and her
memory gone."

I had hoped she would not speak of this;
Jade's face is horrified, and the look he gives me
is one of shock and pity. He will not censure
me, none of my brothers or sisters would censure me; but they would pity me.

"Tell me," Jade says, in a tone that will not
be denied; so I tell him what I can remember,
which is little. And finally, his face white and
sickly, his voice almost smothered beneath the
roar of the crowd which is screaming itself
hoarse because one of Ifania's fighting women
from Gyre has knocked down another swordsman belonging to the Akharet, and knocked
him senseless—in fact, I heard later that he
died of concussion—he manages to say the
words I need to hear. I have blamed myself so
often for submitting, for not defending myself
at the cost of my life. But Jade pats my shoulder with hands that shown no revulsion, and
says very simply, "None of it was your fault.
You did what you must to survive. To take up
the sword in preference to becoming a harlot,
that showed the courage of a warrior. I am
proud to be your brother, Amber."

That almost defeats me, where danger has
not. Jade goes on for some time, exchanging
courtesies with Ifania, begging that he might at
least remunerate her for the bribes which con-

vinced the Akharet to let me go to Ifania's house, which she steadfastly refuses, and at the last I take out the amber earrings I had replaced in my earlobes and beg Ifania to accept them.

"They are the dearest things I possess," I tell her. "They were a gift of love from Beizun, and the only things which are truly my own. Keep them, and whenever you wear them think of Amber."

This makes her cry again, and I know that I will never forget her, and that I will always miss her. But when Beizun returns successfully from her second fight, it is into her arms that I fall, sobbing. In her I part not only from a kind mistress, but from my dearest friend, with whom I have shared dangers and adventures—and love, too.

For her at least I can do something. When I whisper her story to Jade he readily offers to pay the gambling debts which forced her into the arena—the sum is paltry after all, I am shocked at the smallness of the sum, no more than the price of a cheap dress or a small radio—which forced a woman into a choice between harlotry or death.

"So now I am off to Rhadamuth, and my sisters in the guards," Beizun says joyously. But when she sees Ifania's tears, she embraces and comforts her.

"Don't cry, my lady. There are many women fighters, and now you have Kerrak to keep you warm nights," she reminds her. "And now you'll have him all to yourself."

This makes Ifania giggle feebly. As the games end Jade insists I must go out to march with the winners.

"It is your right," he insists, and so for the last time I go out on the sand, hearing for the last time the cries:

"Zadieyek! Zadieyek of Gyre!"

Ifania bids us farewell, and insists on loaning us riding beasts and tents so that we can march into the desert to our rendezvous with the concealed shuttle. Of course she thinks we are going to Gyre, whence she still believes I came. I let her believe it; but when Beizun comes and insists that I must call on Mikhala and give her Beizun's love I tell her the truth—or as much of the truth as she can fathom.

"We are going much farther than Gyre, love."

"I was sure of that," she remarked, "and you will never return."

"No, never."

She kisses the earlobes from which I have taken the amber rings she gave me. She whispers, "Don't forget me." And so I leave with a great gift after all; I had never before this known that Beizun could weep.

13 Strapped and immobile in my gravity-couch, I twist for a last look as the planet, whose name I now know, falls away beneath me. I am remembering the first night in the desert, when Jade and I drew close together before sleep. It made me first giggle, and at last cry, and I had some trouble to explain it to Jade.

"I was thinking of Beizun."

"The woman was your lover; I knew that of course," Jade said gently. "It is a pity she could not come with us; as a fighter she would be an ornament to any sword-group."

"She would neither understand nor believe this—that the women and the men in the group are sworn never to share love," I said. I could hear her now:

"Well, no *wonder* you're crazy, living with

three perfectly good men and not sleeping together! It would make anyone crazy, living like
that!"

But there was no way I could mention that to
Jade. If I did, he would pity me again, or perhaps think I was trying to tempt him to the
breaching of this most ancient of taboos. Dearly
as I love Jade, the thought of doing with him
what I had done without my consent, forced by
the desert bandits, then what I had done at
least willingly with Kerrak almost turns my
stomach. Yet I know he would never offer it,
and if I did he would be revolted and probably
impotent as well, from shock or disgust. It was
a comfort to sleep chastely in his arms as I had
done nights without number.

And now I look my last on the nameless
planet—it has a name only in star-catalogues.
The arena and Zadieyek are now a part of my
past; on that dim dusty world falling away
beneath me I have known terror, pride, strength—
and love. Perhaps, sometime when the hurt has
subsided, I might whisper these things to Emerald, before we sleep; we have been lovers
since before our breasts grew, and she would
understand and perhaps know why I will never
forget. But even from her I would keep a few
secrets. I would tell about the arena, and about
Hassim's gallantry and kindness; about Ifania
and Beizun. But even to her I would never
whisper of Kerrak and the guilty pleasure I
found in his arms.

Only perhaps to Grandmother would I tell

all. She too has known the pain of changing worlds, she has known that for every gain there is loss, and for every loss, however painful, there is something of gain. I have lost my very self, the old Amber, on that unknown world down there, and have found a new self. And as the world vanishes, I realize that within the restored surface of Amber Leontas, there will always be something of Zadieyek of Gyre. And if that is not entirely a good thing, it is not a bad thing either.

But good or bad, I will have to live with them both.

Bestselling SF/Horror

☐ The Brain Eaters	Gary Brandner	£1.95
☐ Family Portrait	Graham Masterton	£2.50
☐ Satan's Snowdrop	Guy N. Smith	£1.95
☐ Malleus Maleficarum	Montague Summers	£4.95
☐ The Devil Rides Out	Dennis Wheatley	£2.95
☐ Cities in Flight	James Blish	£2.95
☐ Stand on Zanzibar	John Brunner	£2.95
☐ 2001: A Space Odyssey	Arthur C. Clarke	£1.95
☐ Elric of Melnibone	Michael Moorcock	£1.95
☐ Gene Wolfe's Book of Days	Gene Wolfe	£2.25
☐ The Shadow of the Torturer	Gene Wolfe	£2.50
☐ Sharra's Exile	Marion Zimmer Bradley	£1.95
☐ The Blackcollar	Timothy Zahn	£1.95

ARROW BOOKS, BOOKSERVICE BY POST, PO BOX 29, DOUGLAS, ISLE OF MAN, BRITISH ISLES

NAME ....

ADDRESS ....

....

....

Please enclose a cheque or postal order made out to Arrow Books Ltd. for the amount due and allow the following for postage and packing.

U.K. CUSTOMERS: Please allow 22p per book to a maximum of £3.00.

B.F.P.O. & EIRE: Please allow 22p per book to a maximum of £3.00.

OVERSEAS CUSTOMERS: Please allow 22p per book.

Whilst every effort is made to keep prices low it is sometimes necessary to increase cover prices at short notice. Arrow Books reserve the right to show new retail prices on covers which may differ from those previously advertised in the text or elsewhere.

Bestselling Fiction

☐ Dancing Bear	Chaim Bermant	£2.95
☐ Hiroshima Joe	Martin Booth	£2.95
☐ 1985	Anthony Burgess	£1.95
☐ The Other Woman	Colette	£1.95
☐ The Manchurian Candidate	Richard Condon	£2.25
☐ Letter to a Child Never Born	Oriana Fallaci	£1.25
☐ Duncton Wood	William Horwood	£3.50
☐ Aztec	Gary Jennings	£3.95
☐ The Journeyer	Gary Jennings	£3.50
☐ The Executioner's Song	Norman Mailer	£3.50
☐ Strumpet City	James Plunkett	£3.50
☐ Admiral	Dudley Pope	£1.95
☐ The Second Lady	Irving Wallace	£2.50
☐ An Unkindness of Ravens	Ruth Rendell	£1.95
☐ The History Man	Malcolm Bradbury	£2.95

ARROW BOOKS, BOOKSERVICE BY POST, PO BOX 29, DOUGLAS, ISLE OF MAN, BRITISH ISLES

NAME ....

ADDRESS ....

....

....

Please enclose a cheque or postal order made out to Arrow Books Ltd. for the amount due and allow the following for postage and packing.

U.K. CUSTOMERS: Please allow 22p per book to a maximum of £3.00.

B.F.P.O. & EIRE: Please allow 22p per book to a maximum of £3.00.

OVERSEAS CUSTOMERS: Please allow 22p per book.

Whilst every effort is made to keep prices low it is sometimes necessary to increase cover prices at short notice. Arrow Books reserve the right to show new retail prices on covers which may differ from those previously advertised in the text or elsewhere.

Bestselling Thriller/Suspense

☐ Voices on the Wind	Evelyn Anthony	£2.50
☐ See You Later, Alligator	William F. Buckley	£2.50
☐ Hell is Always Today	Jack Higgins	£1.75
☐ Brought in Dead	Harry Patterson	£1.95
☐ The Graveyard Shift	Harry Patterson	£1.95
☐ Maxwell's Train	Christopher Hyde	£2.50
☐ Russian Spring	Dennis Jones	£2.50
☐ Nightbloom	Herbert Lieberman	£2.50
☐ Basikasingo	John Matthews	£2.95
☐ The Secret Lovers	Charles McCarry	£2.50
☐ Fletch	Gregory Mcdonald	£1.95
☐ Green Monday	Michael M. Thomas	£2.95
☐ Someone Else's Money	Michael M. Thomas	£2.50
☐ Albatross	Evelyn Anthony	£2.50
☐ The Avenue of the Dead	Evelyn Anthony	£2.50
